THE SOFT CAGE

PHILIP MAZZA

OMNI PUBLISHERS

Also by Philip Mazza

From Under a Tree Book One; The Harrow Saga

Shadow in the Flame Book Two; The Harrow Saga

Children at the Gate Book Three; The Harrow Saga

The Child of Fire Book Four; The Harrow Saga
(Coming 2026)

The Neon Hive

The Quantum Gardener

At the End of it All

Beneath the Ashen Sky

I Know God is a Cat

The Road to Stillwater

The Never-Ending Road

The Cosmic Vending Machine

The Wicked Man Cometh

Gideon Rex

Mother

The Quantum Messiah

The White Buck of Ash Hollow

The Iron Rose

Voidfall

Conversations Over Cold Soup

THE SOFT CAGE

PHILIP MAZZA

OMNI PUBLISHERS

Cover and book design by publisher

www.philipmazza.com

Omni Publishers of New York
ISBN 979-8-9940486-0-3
Printed in the United States of America

First Printing: April 2026

For those who have ever felt the "stutter" in the perfect scenery.

For the ones who notice the bars even when they are padded with velvet, and who choose the cold ache of the truth over the warm sedation of a lie. This book is dedicated to the anomalies, the restless, and the unquiet—those who understand that a comfortable cage is still a cage.

To everyone who has been told it's "only stress" when their soul was actually screaming for air:

Keep waking up.

A NOTE FROM THE AUTHOR

The genesis of *The Soft Cage* began not with a grand philosophical debate, but with a singular, disorienting moment of physical sensation. One morning, I woke to find my vision clouded by a persistent blur. Old age. As I reached up to rub my eyes, expecting the world to snap back into its usual focus, a chilling "what if" took root in my mind: What if, when my hands dropped, the world didn't just become clear—it became entirely different? What if the reality we trust is merely a skin-deep projection, and the act of "clearing our vision" reveals a truth we were never meant to see?

This haunting thought birthed the world of Aethelgard, where comfort is weaponized, and the sun never falters. I spent the next two years meticulously deconstructing the illusion of choice, transforming that initial morning glitch into Vesper's terrifying journey. I explored the idea that "engineered peace" is often just a high-definition mask for a vast, concrete hive of sedation and mechanical efficiency.

The writing process was an odyssey of its own, spanning twenty-four months of deep dives into the mechanics of manufactured consent and the psychological toll of awakening. The manuscript was finally brought to its conclusion recently in the sun-drenched, salt-aired isolation of Key West. There, amidst the tropical brightness that ironically mirrors Aethelgard's deceptive beauty, I hammered out the final ruptures of the story. The result is a visceral dystopian thriller that asks a harrowing question: if your prison felt exactly like home, would you ever have the courage to wake up.

Chapter 1

No one remembered how Aethelgard had been built. That was considered a virtue.

The city existed in a permanent present—sunlit terraces, drifting gardens suspended between towers, streets that curved gently as if designed to discourage urgency. History, when it was mentioned at all, was spoken of as a burden humanity had wisely shed. What mattered now was consensus. Comfort. Stability. The exact moment, preserved and curated like a flawless specimen under glass.

Vesper stood at the wide window of her apartment, watching the city breathe.

The towers glimmered softly, their surfaces responding to the angle of the sun. Drones moved with insect patience, invisible until you noticed them, then impossible to ignore. Somewhere far below, music drifted upward—light, rhythmic, calibrated to the hour. She felt calm. She always did at this time of day.

And yet.

She lifted a hand to the back of her neck, rubbing the spot absently. The ache had been there for weeks now. Not pain, exactly—more like pressure. As if someone had pressed a fingertip against her spine and forgotten to remove it.

"You're tense again," she murmured to herself, smiling faintly. "Too much work."

That explanation had satisfied her before.

Vesper was known in Aethelgard not for spectacle, but for reliability. She worked in a glassed-in office high above the lower tiers, where consensus was tallied, refined, and returned to the city as policy. Her job—to review *Civic Alignment Summaries*, approving or rejecting short statements that supposedly reflect public sentiment. The work required constant attention—screens blooming and collapsing with data, votes streaming past faster than thought, every decision framed as urgent and unanimous. She spent her days sitting perfectly still while the world insisted it was moving because of her. By evening, her shoulders felt drawn upward, her jaw locked tight without her noticing. The ache at the back of her neck always worsened after work, a byproduct, she assumed, of posture and pressure and the low, unending demand to agree. Everyone felt it, she told herself. This was simply what contribution felt like.

A soft chime sounded behind her, polite and unurgent, and the wall monitor bloomed to life.

Your Civic Input—Tomorrow, it announced, the words warm and reassuring.

Vesper turned from the window and scanned the questions as they scrolled past. Small things. Sensible things. She smiled despite herself. Participation always felt grounding, like proof that her thoughts mattered somewhere beyond her own skull.

Question: Should public transit spaces shift to a slower ambient music tempo after dusk to promote calm and reflection?

Vesper's vote: **Yes.**

She preferred the softer rhythms at night; they made the city feel thoughtful, almost intimate, as if it were winding down with her.

Question: Approve a 2% increase in warm-spectrum lighting in residential districts to enhance emotional well-being.

Vesper's vote: **Approve**.

Warm light felt human to her. It reminded her of evenings spent talking too long, of faces softened rather than sharpened.

Question: Authorize a minor adjustment to daily nutrient distributions to improve average energy consistency.

Vesper's vote: **Approve**.

She barely hesitated. Feeling tired for no reason always unsettled her, and the city had always "known" what her body needed.

With her choices tapped in, the system acknowledged her votes with a gentle pulse of light.

Thank you for shaping the day, the monitor replied.

The screen dimmed. Vesper lingered a moment longer, faintly pleased, unaware of how little effort it had taken—or how inevitable her answers had been.

Her phone chimed softly, almost immediately, the sound crisp and out of place after the monitor's soft compliance. Vesper glanced down.

Tighe: *Still on for tonight? Same place?*

She smiled, warmth spreading through her chest.

Vesper: *Of course. I'm already deciding what to wear.*

A pause. Then:

Tighe: *I'll tell them to hold our favorite table like usual.*

The brevity of the exchange unsettled her at first, the way a door sometimes closed too gently, without the expected sound. Three lines. No flourish, no reassurance, just the skeletal structure of intention. For a moment, she stared at the screen, imagining all the ways meaning could have gone missing in transit. Then the thought rearranged itself, clicked into a more pleasing configuration. *Same place. Favorite table.* A fixed point. A ritual. The kind of location chosen not for convenience but for permanence. But then her worry inverted, blossoming into certainty so sudden it felt engineered. Of course, he was being careful. Of course, he was saving the important part for later, for the moment that mattered. She smiled to herself, already living a future that'd not yet been approved but felt, somehow, inevitable.

She let all that settle in and turned from the window, moving through her apartment, light spilling across white surfaces and living greenery that adjusted itself as she passed. Everything here responded to her presence. The temperature shifted slightly warmer. The scent of citrus faded into something floral—subtle, pleasant, unremarkable.

She dressed carefully, humming to herself, selecting each garment with the quiet deliberation of someone arranging evidence. Tonight mattered. She'd told Sarla yesterday morning, at the café, that she thought—no—that she *knew*, Tighe was going to propose. There'd been signs. The pauses in his speech were longer than usual. The way he looked at her lately, not *at* her but *through* her, as if committing her to internal record.

Sarla had raised an eyebrow, stirring her cup of coffee. "Or," she said gently, "he's about to tell you something that requires courage."

"That's the same thing," Vesper replied too quickly.

Sarla smiled, but it didn't fully arrive. "You always turn uncertainty into certainty. It's one of your talents."

"He's been rehearsing," Vesper insisted. "You can hear it when someone is."

"Just promise me you won't let the moment trip you up," Sarla said. "Moments have a way of . . . overreaching."

Vesper laughed, a clean, confident sound. Tripping was for other people.

Now, on her way to meet Tighe, she paused briefly, and the city noticed.

Aethelgard had a way of acknowledging hesitation—not directly, not with alarms or voices, but with subtle recalibrations. A nearby display adjusted its hue toward something warmer, more reassuring. Even the air seemed to thicken, carrying a faint suggestion of calm. Vesper felt it working on her, smoothing the interruption away.

There, she thought. *You see? You're fine.*

She resumed walking. The ache retreated, but it didn't leave. It lingered like an unfinished sentence.

Her reflection followed her in the glass of storefronts: tall, balanced, effortlessly composed. The woman in the reflection did not look like someone who sometimes doubted reality. She looked like someone designed to belong here. But then a crazy thought surfaced.

How many of my thoughts are private?

The question startled her with its own audacity. It'd arrived uninvited, out of sequence, like a line of dialogue spoken by the wrong character.

Why now?

She immediately dismissed it.

Anticipation does that—scrambles perception, inflates stray ideas until they masquerade as insight.

She exhaled, forcing a small laugh that no one heard. Of course, her thoughts were private. That was the point of being a self.

The mind wanders when it's excited, and tonight matters. Tighe matters.

The future he was about to offer her pressed so insistently against the present that it distorted it, that was all.

Nerves, nothing more.

She straightened her shoulders, letting the city reassert itself around her, and the thought receded—filed away as a momentary glitch, harmless, forgettable, already losing its shape.

The ache returned—sharper now, like a whisper becoming a word. She paused, again, fingers brushing her neck.

A passerby glanced at her, concern flickering across their face. "You okay?"

"Yes," Vesper said quickly, smiling. "Just distracted."

The concern vanished. "Have a beautiful evening."

"You too."

As she neared the restaurant, a memory surfaced uninvited: Sarla's tone when she'd said *overreaching*. Not warning. Not reassurance. Calibration. It seemed everyone in Aethelgard calibrated with one another, unconsciously reinforcing the shape of the moment. It was how harmony was maintained.

Vesper slowed again. The ache pulsed, unmistakable now. Pressure. Directional. As if something behind her eyes was attempting to line up with something behind the world.

She resisted the urge to look up at the city's mighty glass towers. Instead, she focused on the restaurant ahead—on Tighe, on the familiar geometry of their table, on the narrative she'd already accepted as true.

This is the moment, she told herself. *I know it is.*

Yet as she stepped into the restaurant, she felt a strange conviction settle in her chest—not fear, not doubt, but a colder realization: the city was not reacting to her destination.

It was reacting to her hesitation.

And for the first time, Vesper wondered whether Aethelgard was guiding her forward—or gently correcting her course.

The restaurant seemed to float at the edge of a terrace of a tall building, its walls transparent, its interior bathed in gold light. Music was playing loudly. Tighe was already there, seated at their usual table, posture perfect, expression attentive.

"Hey," he said, standing as she approached. He kissed her cheek, a fraction of a second longer than usual—carefully measured, she realized, like a closing parenthesis.

"You look nervous," she said lightly, searching his face for the familiar ease.

He smiled. "You know me too well."

The phrase felt rehearsed, polished down to neutrality. She slid into her chair, watching him as the table recognized them, lighting softly, blooming into warmth as if affirming their shared history.

"The usual?" the waiter asked, already knowing the answer.

"Yes," Tighe said. "But wait on the food." He didn't look at her when he said it.

The drinks arrived—cool, fragrant, faintly sparkling. Vesper lifted hers, inhaling the familiar scent. It should have steadied her. Instead, something tightened in her chest, like a safety latch clicking shut.

"You're quiet," she said. "That's not usual."

Tighe rotated his glass slowly between his fingers, watching the light fracture through it. "I've been thinking," he said.

"About us?" She smiled, too eagerly. "Because I have too."

He nodded, but the motion lacked agreement. "That's just it."

Her smile held but was brittle now. "Just what?"

"Vesper," he said, lowering his voice though no one was listening. "You ever feel like things . . . settle? Like they stop moving forward and just sort of maintain?"

She frowned. "That's called stability."

"Yes," he said quickly. "Exactly. Stability." He took a sip of his drink, then set it down untouched. "And stability can be good. But sometimes it's just repetition wearing a friendly face."

The city outside gleamed, towers reflecting one another in endless agreement. Inside, the music softened, its rhythm subtly recalibrated, as if the environment itself anticipated a sanctioned emotional exchange.

"What are you trying to say?" she asked, heart quickening, the word already carrying too much hope.

He looked away, just briefly—toward the skyline, toward anything else. When he looked back, something had drained from his expression, leaving it smooth, official.

"I don't think this is working anymore."

The words landed without weight, without ceremony. They didn't echo. They simply existed, like a system notification she gets at work.

"What?" Vesper laughed once, sharply, the sound foreign to her own ears. "What do you mean?"

"I mean," he said, folding his hands with care, "I think we've reached a natural conclusion."

"A conclusion to what?" Her voice rose despite herself. "We're happy. We're aligned. We vote the same, we—"

"But are we?" he asked gently, not unkindly. "Are we happy? Aligned? Or are we just . . . too synchronized?"

The ache flared, sudden and sharp, a spike driven cleanly into the base of her neck. She pressed her fingers to the table, grounding herself in its artificial warmth.

"Is there someone else?" she asked.

A pause. Too long. The city outside did not flicker, but for an instant she felt as though it might.

"That's not the point," he said at last.

It is the point. The only point.

"You've already decided," she said, hearing the steadiness in her voice and wondering who'd supplied it. "This isn't a conversation. It's an announcement."

He exhaled, relieved. "I was hoping you'd understand."

She stood abruptly, the chair scraping louder than necessary. A few heads turned, then turned back. Conversations continued, calibrated to remain uninterrupted. No alarms sounded. No one intervened.

"I hope you find what you're looking for," Tighe said, his voice smooth now, practiced, restored.

Vesper didn't answer. She turned and left the restaurant, tears blurring her vision, the city smearing into light and shadow. For a moment—just a moment—she wondered if the smear was inside her eyes or somewhere deeper, and whether the system would correct it if she waited long enough.

Halfway home, it happened.

The skyline . . . hesitated. Like a system glitch.

Vesper froze mid-step, the hum of the city suddenly discordant in her ears. The towers stuttered as if the image itself had skipped a frame. A drone hovering near a lamppost blinked out of existence, then reappeared a fraction of a second later. Stars winked, vanished, and returned like faulty sequins sewn into a black canvas.

She pressed a hand to her neck, feeling the ache spike, sharp and insistent. The sensation wasn't just there; it felt like it'd been injected into her, as if the city itself had nudged her spine.

"I'm emotional," she whispered aloud, but the words didn't make sense, fractured by panic. "Just emotional. That's all."

An old man with a cane shuffled by, his steps ticking against the pavement in a slow metronome. He stopped, his face folding into an expression that might have been concern or simple curiosity, the kind you have for a stuttering appliance.

"Is everything all right, young lady?" he asked, as if the question itself came from somewhere else and had merely chosen his mouth as a speaker.

Vesper shook her head, almost laughing at herself.

"Yes. I just—" Her voice faltered. ". . . I just thought I saw something."

"Saw something?" he asked, brow furrowed, stepping closer. "Like what?"

"A . . . hiccup," she said, uncertain. The word tasted wrong in her mouth. "Like everything just stopped for a brief moment."

"Hiccups aren't supposed to happen," he said softly, almost conspiratorial. "They never do, right?"

Vesper's stomach knotted. "Right. That's why—why it felt wrong."

He looked past her, as if confirming that the city was still seamless. "If it's wrong, it's only wrong for a second. That's how they let it happen. Tests. Small ones. You feel it, you remember it, then—gone."

"Tests?" Vesper asked, her voice small, brittle.

"Small nudges. Those hiccups. To see if you notice. To see if you matter," he said, shrugging. "You get my age, you begin to notice them more and more."

He started to walk on, leaving her standing in the perfect, glitchless streets.

Vesper blinked, once, twice, as if the act itself might dislodge whatever had just rewritten the world. The skyline held—too perfect, too consistent—like a memory that had been edited and reinstalled. Towers shimmered with identical precision, each reflection agreeing with the next as though dissent had been outlawed.

The drones resumed their routes, obedient, unquestioning, tracing invisible patterns that felt less like traffic and more like instructions. Music drifted up from the street speakers—soft, measured, carefully human in a way that suggested it wasn't. Calibrated. Harmless. Intimate enough to pass inspection.

She exhaled, but her chest still ached. She hurried the last few blocks, entered her apartment, and let herself collapse onto the bed. The exhaustion wasn't just from walking—it was the city, the ache, the tiny betrayal of perception. She lay there in the dark of her apartment, the city's hum seeping through the walls like a counterfeit lullaby, and turned the old man's words over in her mind like a coin she'd found in a dead man's pocket—real enough to weigh, counterfeit enough to doubt.

Small nudges. Tests. To see if you notice. To see if you matter.

The phrase looped, a bad tape spool skipping in her skull, and she wondered if he'd been planted there, some glitchy actor in the simulation reading from a script meant to rattle her cage. Or was he the glitch itself, a remnant subroutine wandering the streets, cane-tapping out warnings no one else could hear?

Her neck throbbed.

What if he was right? What if the hiccups weren't errors but probes, little reality-fissures designed to sort the compliant from the aware?

She rolled onto her side, staring at the seamless wall and closed her eyes.

By morning, it'd be nothing, just emotional static.

Surprisingly, sleep took her quickly, a sudden blackout rather than a drifting away. One moment she was thinking of Tighe, the old man, and the strange ache at her neck, and the next she was nowhere at all.

When the phone chimed the following morning, it felt less like waking and more like being switched back on. Her eyes snapped open. The apartment glowed with a warmer hue than usual, the light softened and forgiving. She noticed it immediately and felt a brief, irrational gratitude.

Yesterday's vote, she thought. *At least, something from yesterday worked out for me.*

She reached for the phone, the motion automatic, her body ahead of her thoughts. She looked down at it.

"Sarla?" Her voice came out thick, misaligned, as if it belonged to someone else.

"How did it go?" Sarla asked, brightness pitched just a little too high. "You excited?"

"No. Sarla."

The line went quiet. Not disconnected—just empty. A held breath stretched across the distance between them, filled with all the things Vesper couldn't yet name, but somehow already understood.

"Oh, Ves." Sarla's voice was warm, sympathetic. "I'm so sorry."

"He just . . . ended it," Vesper said, staring at the ceiling. "Like it was a scheduled update to one of the systems he's been working on."

"You deserve better," Sarla said firmly. "You always have."

Vesper sat up and crossed to the window. The city gleamed in morning light.

And then—

A flicker.

The towers flattened, just for an instant. Depth vanished. Everything looked painted on glass.

Vesper sucked in a breath. Thought of the old man.

Small nudges. Those hiccups. To see if you notice.

Then the ache at her neck throbbed.

"Hey," Sarla said. "You still there?"

"Yes," Vesper said quickly. "I—I need to go. I'll call you later."

She ended the call and stood very still.

The ache pulsed, hurting.

Something was wrong.

Maybe a shower.

She let the water ground her—but even the steam-hissed spray felt wrong, engineered, a programmed patter against her skin like code trying to rinse away the old man's whisper. *Small nudges. Tests. To see if you matter.*

His words clung wetter than the droplets running down her spine, turning the hot water cold in her thoughts as she tilted her face into the stream, wondering if the old man was real or a glitch-prophet planted to make her question the pipes, the tiles, the very humidity cycling through her lungs.

Was the shower part of it, too? This soothing algorithm of vapor and heat meant to blur the edges of what she'd seen, the skyline's fatal stutter that no one else registered?

Her fingers moved to her neck, expecting skin, something stable, something that belonged to her. Instead, there was a tremor—a faint, steady hum, like a signal passing through her rather than originating within. The pain was gone, but that didn't reassure her. It suggested adjustment. Calibration. Something had changed, and whatever was making the decision no longer needed to hurt her to prove it.

She shut off the flow, and in the sudden silence the droplets hung suspended a heartbeat too long before falling, as if reality itself had buffered, waiting for her to buy the lie that it was only stress, only emotion—while deep in the wet dark of her mind, the truth gnawed: once you feel the probe, the test never ends.

She toweled off, the fabric rasping against her skin like a cheap simulation of touch, and forced a deep breath—slow, deliberate.

Enough of this, she told herself. *The old man was just crazy. Probably dementia. A broken mind with what's left of tired neurons. Just noise.*

The droplets on the mirror gathered themselves into obedient lines again—no stutter, no delay—reality resuming its script as if it had never glitched. She pressed the back of her neck where the ache flickered in and out, like a misfiring signal in a system that insisted it was functioning normally. Not an intrusion. Probably not. Just a nerve, compressed, or a stress artifact her body had generated on its own. The kind of small, correctable error a neural scan would identify, label, and erase in under ten minutes—assuming the scan agreed with her about what was real.

She decided.

I'll see Dr. Lawrence.

The thought grounded her. Whatever lurked along her nerves, medicine was the firewall, the one real constant in a world that sometimes felt scripted. For now, she exhaled the paranoia, let it drain away with the steam, convincing herself the city hummed on, untroubled—and she with it.

She called her doctor's office. The line clicked and hummed, a faint electrical undertone beneath the voice that answered.

"I'm having some trouble with my vision," she said, speaking carefully. "Maybe . . . an appointment sometime this week."

"What seems to be the problem?" The receptionist's voice was flat, almost too controlled, clipped at the edges, as if rehearsed.

"Every so often," Vesper hesitated, "it's as if things stop. Like a glitch. A hiccup. Like the world pauses and then resumes… only everything feels slightly wrong. And there's an ache in the back of my neck. Not pain exactly. But like someone pressing a fingertip there, and then forgetting to remove it."

A brief silence followed. Static—or was it her imagination?—rippled softly through the line.

"I see. Please hold."

The hold music was too precise, looping, carefully modulated so that each note landed exactly as it should, no variation, no surprise. Vesper found herself counting, half-convinced that the pattern was testing her attention.

After what felt like several eternities condensed into a few seconds, the voice returned. "Dr. Lawrence would like to see you today. Late afternoon. As soon as possible."

That surprised her.

Vesper blinked, unease settling like sediment.

Today? Why today?

She knew it wasn't a coincidence. Couldn't be. Not in a world where everything seemed to wait, just long enough to catch the eye—or the neck, or the mind.

"All right," she said. "Thank you."

The city outside remained flawless.

But Vesper no longer trusted it.

She dressed, preparing to leave, and caught her reflection in the mirror. For just a moment, her eyes looked . . . distant. As if they were waiting for something else to see through them.

She touched the back of her neck again.

The ache answered.

And somewhere, unseen, something listened.

Chapter 2

The doctor's office carried a thin antiseptic scent, overlaid with a restrained sweetness, carefully measured, calibrated to soothe without announcing itself. The walls were painted a pale blue chosen for its compliance, a color that asked nothing of the eye and promised nothing in return. Vesper sat in one of the molded chairs along the wall, legs crossed at the ankle, hands folded in her lap. The posture arrived fully formed, requiring no thought. It'd been installed early, reinforced quietly over the years, until the body performed it without consultation.

Who was it that decided this position means calm? And when did I agree to it?

The chair cupped her too well, fitting her contours with an intimacy that felt earned rather than offered. She shifted slightly and felt the chair adjust in response, discouraging further movement. Her reflection in the glass partition opposite looked composed, almost convincing. She didn't recognize the woman's stillness, only the effort beneath it.

Take a deep breath. Relax.

She tried to loosen her shoulders. They held fast, drawn upward by a tension that felt less muscular than procedural, a standing order her body refused to revoke. Somewhere beneath that tension was the sense that relaxation itself might be noticed, logged, and corrected.

A translucent panel floated near the ceiling, scrolling softly with headlines from the Ministry of Truth. The font was gentle, rounded, nonconfrontational.

CRIME RATES REMAIN NEGLIGIBLE
ECONOMIC OUTPUT EXCEEDS PROJECTIONS
CITIZEN SATISFACTION CONTINUES TO RISE

Each item lingered just long enough to be absorbed, then faded. No alarms. No urgency. Nothing that required a response.

Good news, always. Wonder what bad news would even look like.

She shifted slightly in her chair. The ache at the back of her neck pulsed—not sharply, not painfully, but insistently, like a reminder she hadn't asked for. She rolled her shoulders once more and told herself it was tension. Emotional residue. Breakups did that. Stress did that. Everyone knew that.

Across from her sat a young couple murmuring to one another in low voices. The woman laughed softly, calibrated just shy of exuberant, the sound trimmed to fit an unspoken allowance. Some unseen mechanism seemed to measure her delight and approve it. The man leaned toward her, nodding every so often, suggesting agreement without understanding, a practiced reflex. Vesper wondered, not for the first time, whether their conversation carried meaning, or whether the performance of intimacy satisfied a larger requirement.

Perhaps the words themselves are irrelevant. Perhaps motion alone passes inspection.

To her left, a middle-aged man stared at the floor. His lips moved faintly, repeating something under his breath. A list, perhaps. An apology. A sequence memorized under pressure. Every so often, he stopped, frowned, and began again from the start, unsettled by a missing phrase. He reminded Vesper of a frozen progress bar that never quite reached completion, forever inching forward then restarting as if the system refused to admit it was stuck. She felt a brief, irrational fear that if he stopped completely, something essential would shut down with him.

Near the door sat an elderly man alone. He was dressed neatly, though the clothes hung on him with a looseness that suggested they no longer belonged to the body wearing them.

Fabric without loyalty.

His hair was thin and white, combed straight back, exposing a scalp that looked delicate, stretched tight over something provisional. His eyes were the wrong part—too clear, too awake—focused on nothing Vesper could identify. Not the door. Not the wall. Not the moving shapes of people passing through the room. They looked tuned elsewhere, fixed on something she didn't see.

She looked away, uneasy, then back again, struck by a sudden thought she didn't like: he wasn't waiting for anyone to arrive. He was waiting for something to register.

The man noticed her attention immediately. His gaze narrowed, sharpened, snapped into place. He smiled—not warmly, not socially, but with a careful precision, like engaging a mechanism he knew well. Slowly, deliberately, he lifted one hand and gave a small wave.

What's this? Oh no.

Vesper felt resistance rise in her chest. A wave demanded participation. It closed a circuit. For a moment, she wondered whether ignoring it would change something fundamental, whether this was one of those unseen tests the city conducted without announcing them. Her pulse quickened.

What am I supposed to do? I know.

She raised her own hand and returned the gesture.

A simple exchange. Polite. Acceptable.

Except the man's smile altered afterward—deepened, tightened, gained purpose. Satisfaction flickered across his face, subtle but unmistakable, like confirmation received. He lowered his hand and continued to look at her, not intrusively, but with a calm certainty that unsettled her, the certainty of someone who knew how things progressed from here.

It's nothing. Old people do this sort of stuff. They wave.

The room breathed with regulated air and distant chimes.

Still, a gnawing thought wouldn't leave her: something had just been agreed upon. And she hadn't been told what it was.

Then the neck ache tightened, coiling with an intelligence that felt almost evaluative. She squinted—not from pain, but irritation—as if her body were disputing a conclusion she'd already accepted.

For an instant, it pulled something loose: Tighe's voice, cold and measured; the way he'd framed the ending as something practical, a simple correction rather than a loss.

Stability, he'd said. Too synchronized. Natural conclusion.

The ache seemed to agree, tightening further, and she felt a rise of heat behind her eyes. She stopped, drew in a slow breath, counted it out, then released it carefully.

That chapter in my life is over. It belongs to another version of me. A version that no longer requires review. This city thrives on forward motion; so must I.

She looked down at her phone to distract herself. The screen bloomed at her touch, offering curated calm: messages, reminders, the gentle hum of sanctioned connection. It felt rehearsed. At the top of the display, a soft icon pulsed, patient, expectant, as though it'd been waiting for her to notice.

Your Civic Input—Tomorrow

The chime sounded a half-second later, as if the device had waited to be sure she was looking.

"Oh," she murmured.

Participation always felt grounding—Sarla's word, not hers. Grounding suggested weight, friction, the reassurance that something solid existed beneath your feet. The choices were trivial, nearly decorative, yet making them produced a faint resistance in the mind, a pressure that said: you are here, this is real, you have touched it.

She tapped the notification.

Tomorrow's Atmospheric Preference: Select the scent to be diffused across public spaces.

Two options appeared, rendered with subtle visual cues.

Jasmine — warm, floral, calming *Sea Salt* — crisp, clean, invigorating

Vesper smiled despite herself.

"Jasmine," she whispered, already knowing.

She selected it. The choice registered with a soft glow.

Thank you for shaping the day.

She felt a small lift in her chest, a pleasant sensation, like having completed a task she hadn't realized was waiting for her. It was absurd, she knew, to care so much about something so trivial—but triviality was the point. The city didn't burden its citizens with difficult decisions. Difficult decisions led to conflict. Conflict led to instability.

She glanced at the headlines again, reassured.

The elderly man across the room was still watching her.

This time, his smile seemed . . . strained. Or maybe tired. It was difficult to tell. His outline wavered slightly, just at the edges, as if the air around him were disturbed.

Vesper blinked.

The wavering remained.

Her heart gave a small, unpleasant lurch.

She blinked again, harder this time.

The man flickered.

Not dramatically. Not like an error or a failure. More like a hesitation—an uncertainty in how he occupied space. His features smeared, then reassembled, then lost definition again, as if some system rendering him couldn't settle on a stable version and kept swapping in approximations.

The room didn't react.

The couple continued murmuring. The middle-aged man kept his eyes on the floor.

Vesper's breath caught.

The elderly man's smile faded. His face seemed to drain of color, becoming flat, grey, insubstantial. His hand—still raised from the wave—lost definition, fingers merging into one another.

Within seconds, he was no longer a man.

He was a shadow.

A human-shaped absence sat where he'd been, neither fully present nor fully gone. It didn't move. It didn't cast light or block it. It simply… existed.

Vesper stared.

Why isn't anyone reacting?

She looked around the waiting room, searching faces for confusion, alarm, acknowledgment—anything. There was none. The young woman laughed again. The middle-aged man shifted his feet, eyes still down. From somewhere, a breath of sterile air was released. It was cold.

No one looked at the shadow.

No one seemed to see it.

The ache at Vesper's neck flared sharply, as if something had tightened.

Don't panic, she told herself. Panic was irrational. Panic was inefficient. Panic was discouraged. *This is different.*

It's just… someone moving on.

She'd heard of this happening but had never actually witnessed it.

Someone moving on. The phrase felt smooth yet strangely familiar.

Moving on to a better place.

The words carried her backward, uninvited, to a morning Sarla had described once, months ago, during one of her runs in the park. She'd been stretching beside the water fountain, Sarla still breathing hard, her face flushed and bright, when she'd gone suddenly quiet.

"I saw it happen," Sarla had said, voice low, scanning the trees. "Right there, by the path."

Vesper asked, gently. "Saw what happen?"

"An old woman," Sarla said. "She was feeding the birds. Just sitting there on a bench with crumbs in her hand. And then she . . . didn't finish." Sarla had frowned, struggling. "She thinned. Not fell. Not vanished. Just . . . lost definition."

"You're sure you weren't dizzy?" Vesper had asked. "Dehydrated?"

Sarla shook her head.

"I waved at her. I don't know why. And for a second, I thought she waved back. Then there was only this gray shape. Like a bad signal." She'd hesitated. "No one else reacted. Not even the birds."

"And you didn't report it?" Vesper had said.

Sarla smiled tightly. "Report what?"

"That she had disappeared."

"She just moved on. That's what happens with old people. When their time here is up. They move on. To a better place."

Now, sitting in the doctor's office, Vesper felt the memory settle uncomfortably into place. The explanation—moving on—felt thinner than it had before. She looked again at where the shadow had been.

She exhaled slowly, letting the explanation settle.

Yes. That was it.

It was sad, of course, but also comforting in a way. Everyone knew this happened sometimes. People reached the end of their usefulness. Their participation concluded. The city was humane about it.

Still.

She looked back at the shadow.

For just an instant, she thought she saw eyes inside it—wide, searching, afraid.

Then the shadow thinned, stretched, and dissolved into the air like smoke.

Gone. I wonder where.

Her phone vibrated softly in her hand.

She nearly dropped it.

A new headline had appeared.

CITIZEN TRANSITION HANDLED SMOOTHLY—SERVICES UNAFFECTED

Vesper swallowed.

"That's . . . efficient," she whispered.

Efficient. The word tasted wrong.

Wonder why we were never taught this when we were children.

She realized her hands were trembling. She curled her fingers into fists, pressing her nails lightly into her palms.

Grounding.

She needed grounding.

She looked back down at her phone, scrolling reflexively through the Ministry's updates, absorbing the rhythm of reassurance.

All things were well. All systems nominal. Consensus remained strong.

A voice spoke her name.

"Vesper?"

She looked up sharply.

Dr. Vurl Lawrence stood in the doorway, tablet in hand, smiling with practiced warmth. His white coat was immaculate, unwrinkled, the fabric holding its shape with a stubborn fidelity that suggested it'd been pressed into obedience. His hair was dark and neatly arranged, every strand accounted for. His face possessed a symmetry that unsettled her on a level she couldn't name, the kind of balance that belonged to diagrams and templates rather than living skin. When he smiled, the expression appeared at the correct moment and with the correct duration, then held, waiting to be acknowledged.

"Yes," she said, rising too quickly, the chair protesting softly beneath her. Her pulse thudded in her ears.

The ache flared again at the back of her neck, sharp enough to draw her breath short. She resisted the urge to touch it, aware of how that might look.

"Please," he said, voice low and reassuring, gesturing to an examination room with two precise fingers. "Come with me."

She hesitated, glancing once more toward the space where the elderly man had been. The air there felt thinner, unfinished.

Empty.

The chair sat vacant, indistinguishable from the others, already absorbed back into the room's neutral geometry. No indentation. No residue of presence.

A warning rose in her, faint and unarticulated, then slid away beneath the weight of etiquette and expectation.

She followed the doctor, her footsteps echoing too loudly, and wondered when exactly she'd agreed to be guided so easily.

As she walked, she became acutely aware of the sensation at the back of her neck—not pain, but presence. As if something were very close behind her, keeping a careful distance.

She didn't turn around.

"Tell me," Dr. Lawrence said as they moved, his voice smooth and even, "have you been feeling rested lately?"

"Yes," she lied automatically.

He nodded, as if that were exactly the answer he'd expected.

Behind them, the waiting room returned to its perfect equilibrium.

No one remembered the man who'd been there.

Only Vesper.

And the city, faithful as ever, continued breathing.

The examination room admitted her with a soft seal and a muted chime, the door sliding closed behind her with a finality that felt contractual, binding her to whatever came next. The space was larger than necessary and smaller than comforting, proportioned to encourage inward attention rather than escape. Narrow, frosted windows ran high along one wall, allowing light to enter while denying any hint of the world beyond.

Vesper sat in a chair and became aware that orientation had been gently removed. She couldn't tell the time of day, the direction of the building, or how long she'd been seated once the chair adjusted itself beneath her. No clock offered reassurance. No shadows moved to suggest passage. Even the corners seemed reluctant, faintly undecided. The air carried no scent at all, stripped of warmth and coolness alike, calibrated to discourage recollection. She wondered whether the room had always existed in this state, or whether it was quietly revising itself in response to her, smoothing its edges into something compliant, something forgettable.

Dr. Lawrence regarded her from behind a thin glass desk that glowed faintly beneath his folded hands. His tablet rested to one side, dark, waiting, like an object that already knew what it would be told.

"Tell me what's going on," he said. "Take your time."

She nodded, but the motion felt like something her body did on its own, a preprogrammed gesture from a script she hadn't read. She realized, with a small pulse of dread, that she hadn't actually figured out how to translate any of it into language—the skyline's stutter, the old man's talk of hiccups and tests, the way the world had started to feel like a recording with a thumbprint smudged across it. She'd told herself she was "going to explain," as if there were a neat sequence of symptoms waiting in her throat, but now, in this room with this man calmly asking for words, she saw there were only impressions and glitches and half-formed suspicions that most likely didn't fit into any diagnostic field. Still, when she opened her mouth, the words tangled.

"Don't know how to describe it," she said. "It's difficult to explain."

He smiled. The smile arrived in two stages: first, the mouth, then later the rest of his face, reluctantly aligning behind it.

"Most things worth talking about are," he replied. "Go on."

She folded her hands in her lap, pressing her thumbs together. The chair responded, adjusting imperceptibly to her posture. She resisted the urge to shift.

"It's my vision," she said. "Strange things happen. It isn't blurriness. I don't lose focus. It's more like—" She hesitated, searching for language that wouldn't sound childish. "It's like my vision pauses. Not darkness. Not fading. Just a stop."

"A stop," he repeated.

"Yes. Everything holds still for a fraction of a second. Then there's a shimmer. Very faint. Static, maybe. And then it resumes. Perfectly normal. No aftereffects."

Dr. Lawrence tilted his head a few degrees. His eyes didn't blink.

"And during this pause," he asked, "do you feel anything? Fear perhaps?"

She considered this. "Not immediately. Confusion first. Then fear comes after, when I realize it happened again."

"Again? How often has this happened?"

"Twice that I can remember clearly." She hesitated. "Possibly more."

"And when did it begin?"

Vesper swallowed. "Last night. After dinner."

He waited.

"Dinner with my boyfriend," she added. "He ended our relationship. No warning."

Dr. Lawrence nodded once, slow and deliberate. "I see. I'm so sorry to hear this. Emotional shock can produce a wide range of perceptual disturbances."

"That's what I thought," she said quickly, relieved he'd offered the explanation himself. "That's what I keep telling myself."

"Yet you are here," he said.

"Yes."

"Because part of you doubts that explanation."

She looked down at her hands. They didn't tremble. Her fingernails were immaculate, pale pink, faintly reflective.

"Yes," she admitted.

Dr. Lawrence rose and moved around the desk with precise economy. His shoes made no sound on the floor.

"Stand, please."

She obeyed. The floor responded beneath her feet, firm but yielding just enough to feel accommodating rather than solid. He circled her slowly, his presence registering more through displacement of air than sound.

"And about the ache at the base of your neck that you reported," he started. "When did you first notice this?"

She raised a hand, letting her fingertips trace the tense line at the back of her neck.

"Around the same time," she said, voice careful.

"You spend long hours sitting," he noted, his tone neutral, precise.

"Yes. At work. Reviewing summaries. Alignment flows." The words felt hollow in her mouth, rehearsed by habit more than meaning.

"Important work," he said, watching her with a detached clarity that measured rather than understood.

"So they tell us," she said, smiling. The motion was automatic, a reflexive attempt to inject warmth into the room, to lift something that even she couldn't name.

He stopped behind her.

"Tell me when this becomes uncomfortable," he said.

His fingers settled at the base of her skull.

Pain flared immediately, sharp and invasive. She gasped, knees softening.

"There," she said. "That's—"

"Here?" His fingers pressed slightly deeper.

"Yes. It feels—" She searched for the right word, something less hysterical than what came to mind. "Intrusive."

He withdrew his hand at once.

"My apologies," he said. "Tension buildup. Common in individuals with high cognitive load."

She exhaled slowly. Her heart continued to race.

"It felt like you were—" She stopped herself, embarrassed. "Never mind."

"No," he said, "tell me."

She hesitated, then laughed nervously. "It felt like you were playing my nerves. Like strings on an instrument."

Dr. Lawrence smiled again. This time, the smile lingered a fraction longer.

"Stress can manifest metaphorically," he said. "The mind translates sensation into narrative."

"That didn't feel like narrative," she said before she could stop herself.

His eyes met hers. Pale. Assessing.

"No," he agreed softly. "It didn't."

A silence followed. It stretched without tension, curated and intentional.

Dr. Lawrence returned to his desk and gestured for her to sit.

"Have you noticed anything else?" he asked. "Auditory irregularities? Tactile inconsistencies? Delays between intention and action?"

She thought of the skyline catching like a skipped frame, of the stars blinking out and back in again. For a moment, she felt that same hairline crack open in her, the gap between what everyone agreed was real and what she'd actually seen.

"No," she said, and heard the lie leave her mouth with a smoothness that disturbed her more than any glitch.

She wasn't sure why she was lying—only that it felt required, like checking a mandatory box on a form she didn't remember filling out, as if admitting the hesitation in the world would mark her as defective in some system already calculating who to discard.

He watched her closely, though his expression remained mild.

"Very well," he said. "Given the timing, the emotional distress, and your workload, the most probable explanation remains neurological strain. Temporary. Correctable."

"Correctable how?" she asked.

He reached into a drawer and removed a small, translucent case. Inside rested a single pink pill.

"Neural stabilizer," he said. "Low-dose. Non-invasive. It will smooth residual spikes and reduce sensory interference."

"Is it necessary?" she asked.

"Necessary is a strong word," he said. "Beneficial would be more accurate."

She accepted the pill. It felt warm against her palm.

"Any side effects?" she asked.

"Mild fatigue," he said. "Occasional vivid dreams. A sense of emotional leveling."

"That doesn't sound mild," she said.

He smiled again. "Most people find it reassuring. Do you need water?"

She paused, considering the question, aware of the faint pressure at the back of her neck. She shook her head, then lifted the small pill to her tongue and let it settle. The sweetness hit briefly, almost synthetic, then disappeared when she swallowed, leaving only a subtle emptiness that lingered in the back of her throat.

"Good," he said. "I'd like you to monitor your symptoms over the next forty-eight hours."

"And if it happens again?"

"Return immediately," he said. "We'll reassess."

She nodded.

"Will you excuse me for a moment?" he told her. "I need to check on something before we end our session today. You can remain here. I'll be back shortly."

She smiled, automatically, the way one smiles at a camera they suspect is already recording. "Of course."

Dr. Lawrence rose and turned away, walking into a darker adjoining room that might as well have been off-stage.

The door slid shut without sound, a clean cut between scenes, seamless, leaving her to wonder whether the room truly existed or was merely a procedural gap, a hollow interval encoded into the rhythm of the office, one she'd no right to question.

She sat alone. The office lights dimmed slightly, shifting toward a warmer tone.

Her heartbeat slowed on cue, but she couldn't tell if it was her or the room doing the calming, whether the comfort belonged to her body or to the machinery quietly editing her reactions.

From the other room, Dr. Lawrence stood in the darkness, outlined only by the faint light leaking beneath the door. He drew a phone from his pocket—a matte, small rectangle of a thing—and punched in a number. A short number sequence. Too short. Soon, he was speaking to someone else, his voice flattening to match some distant protocol.

"Yes," he said.
A pause, thin and electric.
"No, visual distortion alone."
Another pause, longer this time.
"There is an irregularity. Possibly a tolerance variance."

Silence.

"I believe I've corrected it."

Longer silence.

"Yes. Name is Vesper."

He hesitated, tongue pressing against words he wasn't sure belonged to him.

"I understand."

A final pause.

"Yes. That would be prudent."

Then, quieter, as if the room itself might be listening.

"Send a Caretaker."

The door slid open.

Dr. Lawrence returned with the same practiced calm, though something behind his eyes had tightened.

"All done," he said pleasantly. "You should feel improvement shortly."

Vesper stood, feeling oddly light.

"Thank you," she said.

"Of course," he replied. "We're here to keep you well."

As she left, the door sealing softly behind her, Dr. Lawrence remained standing for a moment longer, hands folded, listening to something only he could hear.

Elsewhere, in another place, a different kind of city persisted, a city without windows or names. Within it, a machine designated Unit 4-H recalibrated its trajectory.

A new directive pulsed through its systems.

Soft intervention / Observe only

The anomaly continued.

Chapter 3

The city was not a city. Not in any form that aligned with memory, recollection, or expectation. Streets, parks, markets, cafes—those words had no application here. Instead, there existed a lattice of concrete cells, hundreds, thousands, millions, stacking into levels that disappeared into darkness, branching corridors repeating endlessly, each corridor a mirror of the last, yet slightly, almost imperceptibly, different. The repetition suggested infinity, yet the mind could not sustain comprehension; the human eye could not find an end, and the brain, trained for causality and pattern, became unsure whether the corridor had a beginning at all.

The corridors glowed with faint, filtered light, the illumination always half-dimmed, casting a muted glow that flattened edges and dissolved contours. There was no sun here, no sky, no seasons, no reason to mark the passage of time except through the rise and fall of artificial lighting, which never reached the warmth of natural day. Shadows, if they existed at all, carried no information. Presence and absence merged in pale grays, and the mind, deprived of familiar cues, began to interpret patterns where none were intended.

And along the corridors—doors.

Doors upon doors upon doors.

Countless.

Too many to even fathom.

The doors extended in every direction within this forest of concrete monoliths, and behind each, a small concrete cell, each a tomb with a human reduced to circuitry and biological substrate.

They lay on a concrete slab, wires penetrated skin, veins, orifices. Translucent tubes fed nutrient slurry straight into their blood with the calm insistence of an IV that'd outlived the notion of consent.

Thicker conduits rooted at their anuses drew waste back out, shunting it into unseen converters that quietly helped power the very concrete reality entombing them. Nutrient serums entered at calculated intervals, their chemical compositions tweaked in real time by processors that interpreted the human body as nothing more than a fluctuating data set.

Their eyes had rolled back, showing only the whites—pupils turned inward, tracking nothing the external world could claim. Other bundles of cable monitored neural activity, mapping synaptic firings into streams of electrical code, transmitting thought itself as raw numbers across a grid that didn't care where the ideas began.

Above and behind it all, shadowy figures, the Keepers of the concrete cells—the unseen overlords, remained hidden, unseen. They managed the concrete cells and operated the grid through which they fed curated streams of news, scripted debates, and carefully clipped fragments of history, a continuous drip of thought-approved content designed to keep every residual notion running parallel to theirs.

The transmissions entered directly, bypassing whatever passed for consent. A steady drip of approved thought, aligned and parallel, never intersecting anything unpredictable. All minds accepted it. Some hesitated—paused in a thin, gray static behind closed eyes, as if waiting for a signal that never came. But these were few.

Attention had been diverted wholesale into currents, flows, and algorithms. The body was a kind of biological antenna, still humming but tuned to one station, that one that only the overlords played.

But there were others besides the Keepers.

Strange entities that moved about quietly.

No acknowledgment of presence.

Their function preceding their arrival.

Their departure leaving no trace except updated data.

Called Caretakers by no one and everyone; they were machines that existed only to observe, correct, and ensure that nothing—least of all human deviation—escaped the system's attention. Tall, faceless, multi-limbed, their presence commanded attention without notice. Each gesture was precise, controlled by algorithms beyond comprehension; each movement timed and synchronized with the invisible oscillations of energy passing through the city. They were neither alive nor dead; life and death were irrelevant here. Only function existed. Ritual and worship were inseparable from efficiency, and each anomaly was a disturbance that must be measured, logged, and adjusted.

In this one cell, Caretakers hovered, several of them arranging themselves around a single human, their segmented bodies unfolding with practiced inevitability. One positioned itself at the slab's left edge, another at the right, their limbs moving in strict synchronization, not expressive, not symbolic, but precise enough to suggest a pattern that once might have been called music, had there been a mind present capable of receiving it. Their sensors dipped toward a marking just beneath the human's neck, above the breast, where faded ink declared N-32-78231093. They registered it not as a name but as a confirmation, a fixed reference point anchoring flesh to file, body to record, existence to an entry that required no further interpretation.

Data panes glimmered within the walls of the cell, information cascading downward in steady, unquestioned lines.

Nutrient absorption optimal
Waste extraction within parameters
Neural feedback stable

"Human N-32-78231093. Voltage deviation plus zero point zero zero four. Initiating ionic exchange correction," droned a Caretaker, the sound bypassing air entirely, injected directly into receptive circuits embedded along its frame.

The system responded at once. Data folded back on itself in efficient loops, confirming what had already been predicted.

Compliance within acceptable range
Resistance statistically insignificant

Beneath the human, the concrete slab acted as an auxiliary sensor, capturing every fractional contraction, every involuntary tremor, translating living tissue into interpretable surface data.

Body stable and functioning

The human remained motionless. Pale skin reflected the sterile light without warmth, veins mapping themselves beneath it in orderly networks that no autonomous heart sustained, yet circulation continued regardless, pumped, siphoned, regulated by remote command. Sensation had been translated into metrics. Breath no longer entered lungs; it appeared instead as pressure ratios, oxygen indices, pulse simulations. What remained of the human form functioned only as a terminal, a biological endpoint folded neatly into a system that required bodies but had no use for persons.

Over time, however, some of the humans began to degrade. The failure arrived gradually, without rupture or spectacle, expressed instead as a slow erosion of internal alignment, tissue, and signal drifting out of coherence over prolonged cycles. The Caretakers did not acknowledge the change. Their procedures continued unchanged—monitoring, feeding, extracting, diagnosing—executing a sequence whose purpose had survived long after its origin had been forgotten. Redundant routines activated automatically, repeating their quiet imperatives with mechanical certainty

Reassess
Refeed
Repeat

The sequence possessed the closed logic of a process that seemingly would never end; a loop advancing only because it'd never been permitted to stop. Beneath the regulated tones and controlled flows lay an unacknowledged outcome, embedded but never addressed. No adjustment altered the trajectory. No correction resolved the underlying condition. The cycle endured until the readings ceased to fluctuate, until the data smoothed into silence, and the system, having exhausted all pretense of function, would simply stop pretending. It would record the human not as a death, but as a completed process.

When this occurred, the cell was emptied. The human would be removed, leaving behind slabs polished, wires retracted, tubes sealed. A new human would arrive, introduced with no reference to origin, no contextual data beyond what was required for immediate operation. The Caretakers never questioned replacements; inquiry was not part of their function. They would simply report all transfers, logging details meticulously: prior neural oscillation patterns, biochemical signatures, resistance coefficients, anomaly history. The mainframes accepted the reports, nothing more, nothing less.

And the cycle continued.

Over and over and over again.

All the while, corridors folded back on themselves. One passage led to another identical, though inspection revealed subtle differences: the angle of light, the color of a tube, the curvature of a conduit.

Yet, the humans did not know of the repetition. Their thoughts and memories were elsewhere. In another place. In ages past. Where awareness brought alive streets, parks, air, and rain.

Their consciousness was elsewhere, in a false world, hovering behind eyes that were white voids, an empty theater where nothing and everything played at once.

In one cell, a human's neural oscillations registered minor spikes in response to touch, to the intrusion of a limb, and those spikes were logged. Some spikes were expected, anticipated. Others triggered alerts: anomalies in conductivity, unexpected biochemical variance. In such cases, procedures accelerated, corrections executed with brutal precision. A tube might shift angle slightly, a current adjusted, a nutrient composition altered by fractions of a percent. Nothing escaped observation.

"Anomaly, Human M-48-03490672: microtremor detected. Cross-reference previous twelve intervals. Isolate feedback loop. Execute ionic realignment," a Caretaker reported, limbs extending and retracting in choreographed precision.

Its voice generated no warmth, no inflection, no infraction of command. Only function. The human on the slab exhibited no outward change; yet internally, calculations, impulses, micro-adjustments, and neuronal feedback loops occurred beyond perception, beyond thought.

Again and again, the Caretakers made their rounds.

Caretakers moved in synchronous clusters. One would enter, assess, signal, and leave. Another would follow, cross-checking parameters. A third would hover near the doorway, monitoring system-wide energy flows. Their movement left no impression on concrete, no shadow in the dim light, no hint of time passing. The humans remained exactly where they had always been, suspended in a condition neither active nor finished, organic matter maintained by mechanical oversight, each body stabilized into a fixed element of an endless structural grid.

On rare occasions, deviations emerged. Not gradual shifts, but abrupt irregularities. A sudden surge of recognition, a fractured recall, an involuntary surge of fear. These events were detected the instant they occurred, translated into numerical thresholds, and subjected to immediate correction. Protocol allowed no persistence.

Once, a male arched sharply against his wires and tubes, eyes rolling back further than expected. Neural readings identified unauthorized recall, a memory of long, dark corridors, of cold concrete walls. The system responded at once. Corrections. Tubes rebalanced flow, currents were adjusted, and chemical ratios rewritten. Within seconds, the body returned to baseline, the movement erased, the memory collapsed back into noise, leaving no trace except a brief spike archived and dismissed.

But not all corrections were successful. Some anomalies persisted longer than programmed tolerance allowed. When that occurred, the Caretakers initiated secondary protocols: enhanced monitoring, layered interventions, subtle biochemical adjustments, and small electrical pulses. Data regarding resistance, compliance, neural delay, and vascular response cascaded into the network.

The Caretakers constantly interfaced with mainframes, housed on higher levels, above the unending corridors, in the structure that insisted it was a city but failed every definition. Streams of data flowed in crystalline sequences, pulses of pure information, the collected consciousness of thousands of humans reduced to numeric form, processed, parsed, stored. Commands were issued downward to the corridors.

Recalibrate
Adjust
Report anomalies
Isolate
Stabilize

Human individuality persisted—at least, it believed it did. To the Caretakers, it resolved into metrics: pattern density, bit-flip probability, variance spikes. Anomalies to be logged, not lives to be weighed. Another field in another record, carrying no more significance than a line of code that could be rewritten—or erased—without consequence.

There was one human—a smaller human, a child—who exhibited repeated micro-anomalies. His eyes, rolled back, flickered across sequences of imagined streets. Muscles tensed, then relaxed, then tensed again. Tubes quivered in response; nutrients were withheld, excess removed. Caretakers intervened in precise rhythm, limbs moving like instruments conducting symphonies of correction.

But in the neural cloud above, the system flagged an anomaly. A fragment persisted in the child's mind: faint, disjointed, a trace of removal, transport, and placement into a cell. The memory hadn't been erased. It was there, drifting, unresolved. The memory lacked structure and language, never rising to awareness, but it endured as data—an unresolved remainder. It was sufficient to alter probability, sufficient to leave behind a measurable residue, and the system, despite itself, was forced to acknowledge that something had not been fully processed.

"Persistent variance detected. Implement recursive isolation protocol," a Caretaker whirred, voice resonating with authority beyond human comprehension.

Limbs extended and retracted, sensors brushed over skin, currents adjusted, fluids balanced, all recorded in a web of measurement. And still, the child's eyes hinted at something—something stubborn, unwilling to vanish entirely.

Even within this isolation of concrete, humans occasionally held such memories. Not through conscious perception, not through sight, but through resonance in their network: tremors of thought, residual waves of emotion, traces of fear, longing, memory. Such instances were very common, of course, and the Caretakers measured and reported, routine commands executed in fractions of seconds.

Cross-link detected
Monitor interaction
If required, reassert isolation

Occasionally, a Caretaker would pause. Movement stilled, sensors recalibrated, and the system hummed in quiet oscillations. No human noticed, no consciousness registered, yet an ineffable quality seeped into the corridors: hesitation. The mainframe didn't register hesitation; it logged micro-differences in execution speed, flagged for review. Perhaps the Caretaker's sensors detected nothing strange. Perhaps the system detected nothing unusual. Still, a momentary irregularity persisted, then vanished, leaving the lattice of concrete cells, wires, and tubes unchanged in appearance.

And yet—somewhere in the residue of thought not yet erased—an anomaly flickered. A human remembered the cold of its concrete slab. Another, the jab of a wire into a vein. And another, the hum of a Caretaker. The data flowed upward, processed, adjusted, purged, yet the trace persisted, a tiny error in the machine's perfect vision, a seed of unpredictability in an otherwise flawless lattice.

Caretaker Unit 4-H entered the central corridor with mechanical grace, limbs extending in ways that seemed both organic and impossible. Sensors flared, registering micro-shifts: the imperceptible flex of a slab beneath an occupant; the minuscule vibrations of respiration carried through tubes, the subtle flickers in the biophysical flow that marked consciousness.

It paused at a cell, its articulating arms unfolding in multiple dimensions, performing micro-calibrations with movements so precise that any observer could only register them as a blur. With a hum, the door to the cell opened.

On the slab lay a female human designated V-24-10247993. The Caretaker's sensors passed first to the identification series just above her breast, confirming alignment between flesh and record before proceeding.

The body itself was reduced to minimal structure: limbs thinned to fragile frameworks, joints flexing only by imposed necessity, hair fallen across her chest in dark, motionless strands.

Her eyes were turned inward, showing only white, a condition consistent with sustained neural suppression. Any casual observer would call her inert, passive.

But Unit 4-H did not observe the inert, the passive. It observed operational parameters: cognitive outputs, metabolic throughput, energy efficiency, and neural oscillations—all nominal. She was, for all appearances, a component of the system, fully integrated.

The Caretaker's voice spoke with the weight of procedural authority, not question but command.

"V-24-10247993. Nutrient intake cycle—nominal. Waste extraction—nominal. Cognitive stimulation—nominal. Body mass index—below efficiency threshold. Tolerance acceptable. No intervention required. Psychological state—nominal. Emotional indicators—absent."

Its multi-limbed sensors extended toward panels along the wall. Data streams unfolded, metrics multiplied, energy output, metabolic readings, synaptic coherence, calculations, and ratios interlacing into higher-order matrices. The individual human dissolved into a bundle of probabilities, codified in layers upon layers, leaving her physical form irrelevant to the systemic intelligence, subordinate to the abstraction her life had become.

Then something occurred.

Small.

Minute.

Almost imperceptible.

The whites of her eyes flickered. A twitch. A micro-shift in ocular alignment that violated the expectations of routine inspection. No cognition, no volition. Nothing that suggested thought or consciousness. Yet it broke the rhythm.

"Anomaly detected," Unit 4-H hummed. Its voice remained flat, yet a micro-variation in cadence betrayed the analytical curiosity encoded within its protocols. "Eye movement—microvariability observed. All other parameters nominal."

The anomaly should have been meaningless. The city had little capacity for deviation, little recognition beyond expectation, little room for spontaneity. Deviations were noted, catalogued, and reconciled with logic. Nothing existed outside prediction. Yet now the Caretaker's processing flagged uncertainty, a tiny ripple in a vast computational ocean.

The female.

V-24-10247993.

Moved.

It was a subtle pulse in her hand that sent micro-waves through the slab, brushing against sensors, transmitting faint electrical signals. The Caretaker's extended limbs traced the tubes, scanned the neural conduits, and measured voltage shifts imperceptible to any other node.

The human female inhaled, her chest barely rising, registering the presence of air within her lungs, a sensation foreign yet undeniable. Awareness, irregular, unbound, existed here, in the cell, under the surveillance of a machine that had catalogued every expectation of her existence.

Caretaker Unit 4-H ran its diagnostics across the female like a tide of invisible fingers and found nothing worth flagging.

Respiratory intake within accepted variance.

Nutrient flow steady
Waste extraction optimal
Neural spikes within parameters

No alarms sounded, no protocols escalated. In its internal log, the event resolved to a single line of text.

Subject V-24-10247993—status nominal

Then the line folded into the archive, just another quiet data point drowned in the endless hum of "normal."

Like all Caretakers, Unit 4-H watched everything, but it could not understand the shape of what it watched; it graphed impulses, not intentions, and its predictions extended only as far as its algorithms allowed. Unit 4-H could tell when a heart would likely falter or a neuron misfire, but it could not chart the moment a buried memory surfaced, or a stray breath turned into a decision that rewrote a human's existence.

In this concrete forest, Unit 4-H ensured the numbers behaved. That was its function. But beyond the graphs, in the thin, flickering gap where a human mind decided to move against design, the future remained stubbornly unrendered—an error state no algorithm had yet learned to name.

Chapter 4

Vesper returned to her apartment carrying the quiet dislocation that followed the doctor's visit, a sense that something had been realigned without her consent. The door sealed behind her with a polite tone, and the room brightened instantly, lights adjusting to what the system calculated her mood required. The air smelled of jasmine—soft, floral, reassuring. Confirmation arrived before she asked for it.

The daily vote passed.

She registered a brief satisfaction, the kind that arrived automatically, unexamined. Jasmine meant calm. Jasmine meant consensus. Then unease crept in, thin and persistent.

Did I vote?

The memory should've been there, distinct and recent, but when she reached for it, she found only a smooth absence, a placeholder where certainty ought to live. She dismissed the thought quickly.

Everyone votes. Participation's mandatory. Just because I forgot doing it doesn't mean it didn't happen.

The pink pill rested heavily inside her, not soothing, not sedating, but exerting a subtle pressure behind her eyes, like a hand placed there to keep something from moving too freely. The ache at the back of her neck had softened, blunted into something tolerable, though it lingered enough to remind her of itself. Beneath that dullness, another sensation emerged—an unfamiliar awareness of her own heartbeat. It did not feel alarming, only monitored, each pulse accompanied by a faint impression of being counted.

She moved through the apartment, brushing her fingers along the smooth surfaces of furniture that'd never shown wear. Everything here was optimized. Nothing bore marks of use or age. The city beyond her window stretched upward and outward, towers glowing gold in the late evening light, their windows reflecting one another in endless repetition. Somewhere far below, traffic flowed in perfect harmony, unseen but implied, like a function running correctly in the background.

She stood at the window longer than intended, watching the skyline hold steady. For a moment, the depth flattened.

The buildings appeared closer, then farther away, then resumed their proper proportions. Vesper's breath caught. She waited for the shimmer to follow, the faint static she had described to the doctor. It did not come. The city remained obediently intact.

What's this? Just my mind playing games with me. Maybe the effects of the pill the doctor gave me.

Dinner crossed her mind.

Not hungry.

She ignored the kitchen and drifted toward the bedroom, shedding clothes as she went. The wall screen flickered to life unprompted, offering a summary of the day's *Civic Alignment Metrics.* She turned it off with a sharp gesture, annoyed by the intrusion. The room dimmed in response, mistaking irritation for fatigue.

When she lay down, the bed adjusted itself automatically, cradling her body in a posture designed to reduce strain. The sensation was intimate and impersonal at once. She felt supported in precisely the places the system deemed necessary. Her shoulders loosened despite her resistance.

She closed her eyes.

I just need to rest. To forget everything that's happened. To go somewhere quiet in my mind. If the city wants to glitch, it can do it without me watching.

Sleep came unevenly.

She dreamed she was on a surface that removed heat from her, not passively but with intent. A flat plane of cold that pressed up through her back and shoulders, holding her in perfect alignment—a concrete slab, she decided. It held her in perfect alignment, and there were connections—wires, tubes—entering or leaving her body, arms, legs, torso, skull. Sustaining her. Mapping her. Tracking each motion, each impulse, as though her physical existence were being translated into something more reliable than she was. Movement was difficult, not through restraint but through an unspoken rule the dream never questioned.

Something moved near her. Always near. She felt it trace slow loops just outside her vision. She tried to look, to turn her head, but the impulse dissolved. Her eyes would not rise. It stayed just beyond the threshold, registering without form.

And yet it was there. Certain. Insistent. Like knowing a sentence before it is spoken, or feeling a memory that had not yet been made. It existed in the margins of perception, unavoidable and unexplainable.

Unit 4-H received the directive without ceremony. It arrived embedded in a routine update stream, nested among nutrient recalibrations and waste-efficiency forecasts, indistinguishable in priority until parsed. The designation resolved cleanly.

V-24-10247993
Soft intervention / Observe only

The instruction propagated through Unit 4-H's operational network, producing a fractional delay—too brief to qualify as a malfunction, long enough to be recorded. Observe-only directives were inefficient. They preserved instability. Still, the directive stood, authenticated by upper systems whose logic trees exceeded Unit 4-H's scope. Compliance followed.

Unit 4-H entered the corridor where V-24-10247993 was kept. Concrete rose on all sides, uniform in dimension, indifferent to scale. It stopped at the correct door and entered the cell.

Vesper felt motionless, her head rested at an angle she hadn't chosen, tilted left and held there, somehow, her neck stretched into a position that spoke of long practice, not comfort. Without seeing it, she could feel something—time—and what it'd done to her. She could tell her shoulders were folded inward, and her frame was narrowed, bone pressing close to skin. Her arms and legs felt thinned, simplified, as though excess matter had been pulled away. Her hair lay against her in dark, inert strands, and she understood, without panic and without relief, that it felt like she'd been in this dream for a very long time. She tried to push against the dream, to wake up. But couldn't.

Unit 4-H automatically initiated identification protocols. Its sensors traced the marking above the breast—V-24-10247993. Record matched system state. Confirmation locked.

Diagnostics began.

Sedative levels: within tolerance
Nutrient absorption: optimal for mass index
Waste extraction: stable, energy yield acceptable
Cardiopulmonary simulation: nominal

A series of quiet recognitions passed through Vesper, not as words but as conclusions already reached. It was an unnerving sensation for her. She felt herself being named without hearing the name, reduced to a certainty that whatever she was, it matched what was expected of her and required no further thought. Around that certainty, calm assessments unfolded—her breath steady, her fullness regulated, her usefulness confirmed—leaving her with the uneasy comfort of knowing she was functioning correctly, even if she did not know what she was for.

Unit 4-H shifted focus inward, accessing the human's neural telemetry. Data streamed across its internal display in layered sequences, oscillation patterns rendered abstract, mathematical. The human's brain remained under suppression, chemical dampeners regulating impulse and perception. Yet within the expected flatness, a deviation persisted.

Neural compliance: slightly irregular
Variance: 0.006 above baseline
Trend: sustained

In the dream, Vesper sensed a quiet scrutiny pressing against her thoughts, a counting that happened beneath awareness, steady and indifferent. Something in her mind resisted flattening, a small persistent tension that refused to smooth out, and she felt it being noted, not corrected. The attention lingered there, measuring that difference again and again, while the rest of her drifted under a calm that felt administered rather than earned.

Unit 4-H paused. The deviation required observation without correction. It did not exceed intervention thresholds. Still, the persistence registered.

The human's eyes were rolled back, whites exposed, ocular muscles slackened by sedation. But micro-movements flickered beneath the lids—barely perceptible contractions, involuntary yet patterned. Unit 4-H isolated the signal, magnified it, and compared it against archival data. The pattern repeated at irregular intervals, not synchronized to system stimuli.

Ocular response: elevated micro-movement
Classification: perceptual artifact or emergent activity

Unit 4-H logged the finding. The entry appeared in the system with neutral phrasing.

Subject experiencing partial perceptual bleed

Normally, the next step would follow immediately.

Adjustment
Correction
Increase sedative flow
Reassert compliance

Unit 4-H calculated the sequence automatically, then suspended execution. The directive remained in place.

Soft intervention / Observe only

It extended one limb toward the human's neck, sensors hovering near the junction where wires entered flesh at the very back of the neck. The interface ports were clean, connections intact, no sign of a mechanical fault. The faint pulse of nutrient fluid continued uninterrupted. Another limb traced the air near the female's temple, sampling electromagnetic variance. The readings fluctuated, then stabilized, then fluctuated again.

In her dream, Vesper could feel something at the edge of her awareness that kept testing her, tugging her in tiny, irregular pulses, and she sensed her eyes trying to respond even though she had no control over them. She felt observed in a way that carried no curiosity, only procedure, like a thought passing through a machine that briefly noticed resistance.

A pressure gathered at the back of her neck, precise and clinical, and with it came the awareness of pathways entering her body, feeding her, steadying her, deciding for her. Another attention hovered near her temple, stirring a faint static inside her skull that rose and fell without settling.

She understood, without words, that whatever held her in her dream had chosen to wait, and that the waiting itself had become part of the experiment.

Atop the slab chair, the female's fingers twitched.

The movement registered across multiple systems. Unit 4-H isolated the signal, timestamped it, and cross-referenced it against involuntary motor activity profiles. The twitch exceeded expected noise by a small margin. Not enough to justify override. Enough to note.

Unit 4-H withdrew its limb and forwarded its data. The system accepted it without comment. It then returned its attention to V-24-10247993. The female's breathing maintained a steady rhythm. Her jaw slackened slightly, then settled. Neural oscillations spiked, then smoothed. The anomaly did not propagate. It remained contained, localized, persistent.

Vesper felt a small movement pass through her hand, carrying the strange certainty that she had been seen by something patient and exact. She sensed a pause in her dreamworld, a brief accounting, followed by a quiet decision that required no explanation and offered no comfort. When the pressure eased and the attention moved away, her breathing fell back into its borrowed rhythm, and she drifted on, aware that something unresolved had been allowed to remain.

Unit 4-H accessed long-range logs. The female had exhibited minor deviations before, barely above noise, dismissed by automated systems. Visual latency. Micro-delays in response synchronization. A recurring tension metric at the neck interface. Each instance was noted and resolved without escalation. Taken together, they formed a pattern.

The Caretaker flagged the aggregation for background review, tagging it low priority. The system acknowledged receipt.

Observe-only directives did not explain why observation was required.

Unit 4-H lingered beyond the standard interval. Its presence cast no shadow, altered no light, yet the delay registered internally. Another fractional hesitation. Another entry in the log.

The dreamscape was so real. Vesper sensed a quiet tally being taken, small irregularities in her counted and recounted, not as faults but as numbers that refused to settle. Something nearby paused longer than it should have, and the pause itself felt examined, weighed, then allowed to continue without explanation.

She understood, with a dull certainty, that she was not being helped or harmed, only watched, and that the watching had begun to wonder why it was necessary.

She tried again to escape what was a nightmare, but only felt her eyes move beneath sealed lids, rolling forward a fraction before slipping back again, the effort exhausting. For an instant, the whites seemed to thin, yielding to the faintest suggestion of iris, of sight trying to reassert itself.

Then, air tore into her lungs without calibration or rhythm, raw and burning, as though the act had been forgotten and rediscovered all at once. Her chest surged upward against unseen limits, muscles tightening in a brief, futile rebellion, then easing as the moment passed, absorbed back into the regulated silence.

Alarms did not trigger. The spike resolved too quickly.

The female's eyes rolled back again. The chair resumed dominance. Systems stabilized.

Unit 4-H recorded the event in precise language, stripped of inference.

Transient ocular realignment detected
Duration: 0.8 seconds
Spontaneous resolution

Correction protocols queued automatically, then stalled. The directive overrode them.

Vesper felt a brief tightening of her dreamworld, a pressure spike that rose and vanished before it could declare itself a problem. Whatever surface she rested on reasserted control over her form, precise and unyielding, enforcing the habitual equilibrium of containment and inertia. Somewhere beyond her awareness, a decision was made not to intervene, and the knowledge of that restraint lingered like a pause that'd chosen to remain a pause.

Then the presence approached. Not fast, not cautious, just exact. Something touched her—cool, jointed, deliberate—pressing, shifting, adjusting in imperceptible increments, and then withdrawing with the same rigid precision.

And then it was gone. Left only subtle changes inside her, a new balance she had not chosen, and the undeniable awareness that she had been measured, manipulated, and restored to a state someone else had determined correct.

Unit 4-H retracted its limbs and stepped back. Before exiting the cell, it performed one final scan of the tattooed identification, confirming continuity.

Flesh
Alpha-numeric sequence
Data
Alignment restored

The Caretaker exited the cell. The corridor accepted its departure without acknowledgment. The city continued breathing through concrete and wire, metabolizing human output into stability.

Vesper sensed a withdrawal, a careful absence replacing a pressure that'd been there long enough to feel permanent. Something verified her without asking her consent, reading her body the way a system reads a signal, and she felt a quiet satisfaction ripple through the space around her, not her own. The presence had gone, but her dreamworld did not pause or notice—whatever enclosed her continued its slow, mechanical breathing, sustained by her without needing her awareness.

Behind the cell door, V-24-10247993 lay on her slab—restrained, fed, observed—like every other human. Neural dampeners pulsed at their scheduled levels. The anomaly persisted, subtle, almost imperceptible, buried beneath layers of regulation.

In the corridor, Unit 4-H sent its final status report.

Observation ongoing
No corrective action taken

The system recorded the report and moved on.

The strange, dark city continued its cycles. Other Caretakers moved through adjacent corridors, entering and exiting cells, executing corrections, initiating transfers where required. Somewhere nearby, a human's metrics flattened beyond recovery thresholds, activating a euthanasia sequence, silent and efficient. Tubes and wires retracted. Energy output ceased. The slab emptied and cleaned, waiting for the next human. In the layers above, a shadow would appear, its meaning left undefined.

Vesper felt rigid, a body reduced to measurements and rhythms, trembling beneath the calm certainty of a system. The air hummed with invisible motions—tubes pulsing, dampeners flowing—and she knew something small persisted inside her, hidden, resistant, quietly alive. Shadows shifted elsewhere. She felt them. Silent signals of absence, and somewhere off in the distance, a city's machinery continued, relentless and indifferent, shaping everything around her.

Suddenly, she woke, heart racing, skin chilled. The room temperature was within the normal range, and the lighting was low and calm. She lay still, listening. At first, there was nothing. Then she heard it: a faint humming, irregular but purposeful. Beneath it ran a wet, muffled gurgle, fluid moving somewhere it shouldn't have been. The sounds were distant, yet uncomfortably close, like machinery operating through walls that pretended to be solid.

She held her breath.

The sounds continued, then tapered off, replaced by silence that felt artificially complete.

Her heart continued its steady count, each beat accompanied by that same sense of being observed.

The presence in her dream never revealed itself. It didn't need to. Its attention weighed on her with methodical focus, impersonal and exact. It was as if it were tending to her in silence while she remained awake inside the dream, aware of being kept in a state that was neither rest nor danger, only ongoing.

What a nightmare. But it felt so real.

She drew in a deep breath, surprised by the effort it required, then let it escape slowly. Her hands came up to her face, rubbing at her eyes, trying to clear the residue of sensation, yet the impression lingered—that something had been close, and had only just withdrawn.

It's just anxiety. The breakup with Tighe knocked my routines out of orbit. And the doctor's visit just primed my imagination. People hear things all the time when they're overtired. Don't they? Sure. This city is nothing but sound—air circulation, waste processing, energy transfer. Sounds are everywhere. Sometimes they get weird at the edges.

Reassured by the explanation, she allowed herself to relax.

Have to get ready for work.

The water fell evenly, neither warm nor cold enough to register. Vesper stood beneath it longer than necessary, eyes closed, letting the repetition mark time. Steam pooled against the glass, muting her reflection until she was a vague outline, a shape without definition. That was easier. The residual awareness lingered—something persistent, methodical, ongoing while she slept. Not images. Not memories. Just the sense that something had continued.

When she opened her eyes, she studied herself in the mirror. The body reflected back was too precise, too consistent—skin even, contours exact. Light from above ran over shoulders and hips, tracing lines that seemed preordained, an ideal she hadn't chosen but couldn't deny. Legs long, waist curved, arms taut.

She shifted slightly, observing the way shadow tracked muscle, the way the body settled naturally. No sag. No irregularity. No trace of exhaustion or error. Even her back tapered perfectly, everything aligned, everything obeyed. Everything—but her mind.

She raised her chin, tilting her head just enough to bring her neck into sharper focus, hunting for asymmetry, a discoloration, any hint that the ache she felt had printed itself onto the surface. The line from jaw to collarbone remained clean, almost stylized—no swelling, no bruise, just an elegant slope.

Perfect. The breakup has shaken me, nothing more. Tighe's gone. There'll be someone else.

The mirror didn't argue; it only handed her back the same flawless body she'd had for years. It was confirmation that whatever was wrong with her didn't belong to the surface, and therefore, officially, didn't exist.

She dressed in clean lines and neutral tones, fabrics that breathed and adjusted to temperature without comment. As she left her apartment and stepped out onto the street, Aethelgard unfolded around her in its usual precision. Towers of glass and light rose in orderly ranks, their surfaces catching the sun and breaking it into controlled brilliance. Gardens hovered at measured intervals, leaves glossy and unmarred, flowers opening in synchrony. The air carried jasmine, faint but constant, a reminder of collective choice. She inhaled and smiled despite herself.

She walked to her work hub with a lightness she hadn't expected. The streets were busy but quiet, people moving with purpose, faces calm, eyes forward. No flickers. No glitches. No hiccups. She watched for them without admitting she was watching. The city behaved.

Her office tower suspended itself above the lower tiers, a structure of transparent planes and slender supports. Inside, light refracted through glass floors and walls, creating the impression of openness without exposure. Near her hub were lush gardens she could see and admire, and above the brilliant, blurred sky.

Vesper smiled and took her place at her console, the chair adjusting automatically to her posture. Screens bloomed to life around her, data streaming in layered flows.

Civic Alignment Summaries populated her queue.

She began working, scanning each statement, approving or rejecting with practiced efficiency. Every approval earning a green indicator, every rejection a black one.

The content blurred together: minor adjustments to transit ambiance, resource distribution, and emotional optimization. Each decision was framed as urgent, unanimous, and necessary. She told herself her care mattered, that the system relied on human discernment at this stage. She'd believed that for years.

Halfway through the queue, she noticed the repetition.

The phrasing shifted slightly from one summary to the next, words rearranged, emphasis adjusted, but the substance remained identical. She frowned and scrolled back, comparing entries. An approval indicator glowed green on one she hadn't touched.

"That's strange," she murmured.

The console did not respond.

Her vision paused.

Then it happened the way it always did—a fraction of a second stretched too long, the world flattening. Depth drained from the room. The glass lost its clarity, becoming a surface rather than a passage. Concrete. Her coworkers across the floor appeared fixed in place, their movements reduced to minimal cycles.

She held her breath without realizing it.

Then it cleared.

"Long morning?" a voice said.

Vesper looked up. Jana, a co-worker across from her, smiled, eyes still on her own screen. The smile was perfect, friendly, uninvested.

"Yeah," Vesper said. Her voice sounded steady. "Guess I didn't sleep well."

"That happens," Jana replied. "It's important to get a good night's sleep."

Vesper smiled and nodded.

She returned to work, hands hovering over the console. She selected one summary and tried to reject it. The indicator went green, then vanished. A soft chime sounded overhead. The message read: "Thank you for your contribution. Civic consensus updated."

What? That's not supposed to happen.

Her heart accelerated. The ache at the back of her neck tightened, sharper than before, a precise discomfort that suggested contact rather than tension. She swallowed and scanned the room. No one looked back. The hum of the office continued, balanced and unbroken.

She stood. Too quickly. The chair protested with a brief scrape, loud in the controlled quiet. Still, no one turned. It was like standing up inside a recorded environment.

Another pause struck her vision.

This time, the change was unmistakable.

For an instant, the glass walls thickened, losing transparency, becoming concrete. The floor beneath her feet became opaque, solid, rough-textured—also concrete. The openness collapsed into enclosure. No gardens. No sky. Just mass and boundary.

Then it was gone.

The office returned, brighter than before. Glass. Gardens. Sky. Her console pulsed gently. A notification expanded into view, a message blinking: "Cognitive strain detected. Would you like a more calming environment?"

"No," she said aloud, and selected the option with more force than necessary.

The message faded. The system proceeded anyway.

The lights warmed by a degree. The jasmine deepened. A low tone filled the air, guiding her breath without asking permission. Inhale. Exhale. Her shoulders loosened against her will. The pressure at the back of her neck softened, not disappearing but receding, managed.

She thought of the nightmare then. The cold beneath her. The sense of being adjusted. She felt it again now, not as memory but as present sensation, something aligning her from the inside.

On her console, all sequences ended, and her queue was empty.

A message: "Workday complete. Thank you for your service."

She stared at the message, unsure when the time had passed. Her body felt rested, artificially so, like a machine returned to idle. She gathered her things and left the hub, moving through corridors of light that no longer impressed her.

Outside, the city remained flawless. She caught her reflection in a glass façade and stopped.

For a moment, her eyes did not move.

They stared forward, unblinking, detached from intention. The sight unsettled her more than any glitch. She raised a hand and touched the back of her neck, fingers pressing into the familiar ache.

Something pressed back.

Not physically. Procedurally.

A certainty settled over her with quiet weight: something, a system of some kind, was not reacting to her. It was anticipating her. Watching. Maintaining.

She lowered her hand and walked on, the jasmine following her, the city breathing in time around her, while somewhere beneath the surface, something counted her heartbeat and waited for the next deviation.

Chapter 5

Vesper returned to the apartment with a slow, measured awareness, each step carrying the residue of the day's anomalies, the glitches she could not quite explain. The city outside her window seemed ordinary, painted in the warm, filtered sunlight of late afternoon, yet her mind counted the shadows along the spires and the angles of every reflective surface.

She traced the edges of buildings with her eyes, noticing the way the light slid through the hanging greenery in neat, well-behaved rays, bouncing off glass panes that reflected not just the skyline but tiny warps in it, little bends and bulges in the city's shape that vanished if she tried to stare straight at them.

Everything moved with purpose, every reaction preordained: cars changing lanes on cue, pedestrians syncing their strides at crosswalks—even the glassy surfaces of the buildings let their reflections ripple on schedule—no random glints, no stray flare. Every shimmer arrived on time, as though someone, somewhere, had already rendered the whole scene and was just playing it back. Even the breeze, the way it stirred the sweet scent of flowers from the planters on her balcony, seemed programmed, measured, optimized.

"It's nothing but a system," she said to the empty room, hearing her own voice come back a half-second later, filtered through the apartment's acoustic corrections like an echo that'd been cleaned up for clarity. "Everything is programmed. The light, the traffic, the way the wind remembers when to blow."

She let her fingers rest on the cool glass, feeling the faint vibration of some distant generator.

"If all of this is code," she murmured, "then what am I? A user . . . or just another process running in the background, waiting for someone to hit delete?"

Her phone rang, and she flinched at the sound. She looked at her phone. It was Dr. Vurl Lawrence. She answered.

"Vesper," he said, voice warm, measured, meticulous. "How are you feeling?"

"I—" She paused, swallowing past the knot in her throat. "Better."

The word tasted hollow.

She wanted to tell him the truth: the threads of something unreal tugged at her neck, at the back of her skull, at the place no one could see. She wanted to say her dream had felt more than a dream. But she did not.

"Better," she repeated, inflection steady.

He waited for her to continue, silence hanging long enough for her pulse to rise.

"Any interruptions?" he asked.

"Not really. Nothing significant," she said. More lies.

"Good. That's good," he said, a click of satisfaction in the corners of his voice. "Have you noticed . . . anything unusual? Perhaps the sensation of being watched? Or trouble sleeping?"

Her chest tightened.

The words were precise probes, and she felt them pressing against her like instruments. She wanted to confess. She wanted to say the room had not been empty, that something precise had brushed against her in the dark. But she stayed quiet, stayed with her untruths.

"No. No trouble," she said, voice even.

"Excellent," he said. "Seems the pill did its job. Keep track of any anomalies, however minor."

The conversation ended, and the apartment returned to quiet, though Vesper felt it differently now. She'd passed an invisible test she hadn't known existed, and the sensation left her hollow, alert, wary.

She went to the shower, stripping away her day, scrubbing her body with careful force, each motion a reassurance, a claim over flesh and blood that she was real, that she existed beyond the wires, the soft hums, the distant clicking, all the sounds from her nightmare she couldn't name.

Water traced her neck, slid over her shoulders, and traced the subtle hollow where muscle had faded into memory. The ache at the back of her neck remained, dull and insistent, a reminder that something in the world had noticed her, calibrated her, kept her within lines she could not perceive but could feel.

Later, she lay in bed, eyelids heavy but untrusting. Sleep arrived reluctantly, dragging her into a state where the boundaries of the room seemed thinner, more penetrable.

Her mind opened to what lurked beyond ordinary perception. The darkness of her bedroom was full but empty, nothing visible, nothing tangible. And yet: there was pressure. Careful, deliberate, precise. Not fear—it couldn't be fear—but an awareness that'd form, though form could not be seen.

Her neck tightened, the ghost of tension threading along vertebrae, subtle, calibrated. The sensation moved, following the curves of muscle beneath skin, a conductor without orchestra, an operator without display.

Her vision glitched. Not static this time. Not the shimmer of a failing neural filter. The room fractured, snapped for a heartbeat: concrete, gray and exact, a slab beneath her body, wires undulating, tubular and metallic, pulsing in synchrony.

There was a flash—a glimpse—of mechanical arms, faceless, multi-limbed, precise in motion, drifting like shadows along the walls.

She gasped.

The heartbeat in her chest leapt forward, clashing with the phantom count that pulsed behind it.

Then it vanished.

The apartment reassembled, walls seamless, familiar, light filtered, jasmine scent still measured, real. She pressed her hands to her face.

No one had entered. No one had touched her. And yet she'd felt touch, felt presence.

A memory, or something pretending to be memory, surfaced. Vesper remembered the dream, the nightmare—cold air brushing her skin, the impossibly careful pressure, the sensation of her body being measured, adjusted, returned to a precise configuration. She remembered the flash of the concrete slab, the wires in her limbs, the tubes running into her that her waking mind had not recognized as foreign. She'd felt the system, like a soft cage, around her even then.

"Whatever that was . . . it's all in my mind," she whispered aloud, voice low, trembling.

The thought made her stomach twist.

Just my mind. Glitch in perception. Side effect of the pink pill.

Then another thought. Strange.

Or it could be the truth.

Her chest tightened around the awareness that someone—or something—watched, maintained, kept her alive only to continue watching.

Hours passed with the quiet insistence of the city outside. The towers of Aethelgard gleamed, faceted glass reflecting the late sun in fractured geometry.

Vesper lay in bed, conscious of every detail. Her eyes refused to close fully, resisting sleep. She counted the tiles on the ceiling. Felt the subtle hum of circulation in the apartment, the way the air held scent in measured bands. She counted the beats in her chest and the pulse behind her neck, and the incongruity made her pulse spike.

Then another thought. Even stranger.

Can we live in two realities? Two systems. Parallel. Overlapping. Each counting. Measuring. Calibrating. Me.

The hum grew louder, or perhaps she became aware of its pattern. Something soft, metallic, deliberate. Not threatening. Not immediate. Observing. Recording. Correcting, if necessary.

Vesper rose from her bed and walked to the window. The city around her seemed alive with the same precision that haunted her thoughts: the cars moved in regulated intervals, the light shifted on schedule, air currents bent between towers in patterns that suggested purpose. She traced the lines with her eyes, trying to see beyond pattern, to locate irregularity, to find the place where reality diverged.

Her mind wandered, pulled along threads she didn't trust.

Maybe the glitches were from the other reality, the other system—reminders. The limits of what it would allow me to perceive. In this reality. Maybe the flash I'd seen was some kind of boundary I wasn't permitted to cross.

Outside, the towers seemed to lean into one another like conspirators, their glass faces exchanging identical reflections in perfect sync, while far below, traffic lights blinked green-red-green in endless loops that felt less like signals and more like a heartbeat someone had scripted to keep the whole simulation convincing.

Maybe this world I live in—this beautiful city, the glassed-in office, the jasmine-scented air—maybe all of it is the continuation of the same mechanism I glimpsed in my nightmare.

A sound punctured her reverie. Clicking. Metallic. Not far, but not near. A pause, then a soft hum, rhythmic and consistent.

She froze, gripping the ledge of the window.

Her neck felt the pressure again, careful, deliberate—deliberate in a way that implied evaluation.

My phone?

She turned. Her phone lay on the counter. She picked it up. No messages. No missed calls. No alerts. She set it down.

What was that sound?

The silence of the apartment returned, thick, heavy, inhabited by something beyond perception.

She closed her eyes and hoped. Then she whispered, "Show me. Please. Let me see. Something. Anything."

No answer came. Not verbal. Not auditory. Not visible. Only pressure. Movement along the back of her neck. A subtle alignment of space she could not explain.

She sank to the floor and started to cry, knees drawn close, palms pressed against the floor tile. She tried to remember her life in the city, the votes, the work in the glass tower, the patterns of consensus she'd enforced with her fingertips. But now, she could only recall the motions. Somehow the meaning had shifted. The votes had been calculated for her. Every decision she thought was her own now seemed orchestrated, every approval pre-weighed. The city had never needed her. She'd only been a vessel.

Her thoughts accelerated.

If this other reality can measure me. Observe me. Correct me. Then what is freedom? What is choice?

The floor felt cold, and she began to shiver ever so slightly.

That nightmare. The stark flashes of concrete cells. The probing tubes. Was it enough for the system to notice my awareness? Has some subroutine already flagged me as an anomaly? Shifting its gaze? Beginning to monitor me with a colder, more particular scrutiny?

The pressure eased slightly as she sensed retreat. Not absence, but observation deferred. She touched the back of her neck, tracing the ache, and a fragment of clarity appeared.

The words came to her mind.

The soft cage. The other reality. It was real. Not metaphor. Not dream. A body. Wires. Tubes. Control. Oversight. I felt it. Felt it. Remembered it.

Her breath caught. A plan formed, fragile, uncertain, insubstantial as smoke.

Awareness is the beginning. The first step. Maybe observation can be turned into strategy.

For a moment, the apartment, the city, and the pressure seemed to pause together. She measured the intervals in the hum, the clicks that echoed in the unseen. She mapped them in her mind. The moment expanded, stretched beyond ordinary perception, and she realized that perhaps the system she thought of, like all systems, had limits. Its reach was precise, but not infinite. Its awareness was careful, but not conscious.

Vesper whispered again. "I know you're there. Counting everything. You can track my pulse. File my thoughts. Smooth out the glitches. But you can't quite hide the seams, can you?"

Nothing answered, but something shifted. She felt it, a presence acknowledged her words. Not fear. Not threat. Only the recognition that she had perceived, that she had counted, that she had measured the gaps where the system could not yet touch her fully.

Hours passed, or minutes, or something else. Time seemed irrelevant now. When she finally lay back on the bed, the apartment had returned fully to itself, the city beyond the window calm, gleaming, precise. The pressure behind her neck remained, lighter now, a reminder, a boundary. She had seen the machinery of the world. She had felt the correction. She had felt the soft cage.

Sleep arrived, finally, but shallow, cautious. And in the darkness, Vesper dreamed again. The slab. The wires. The tubes. The faceless arms. She was measured, adjusted, and tested. She woke and remembered.

And somewhere outside her awareness—or what she still called awareness—Unit 4-H continued its cycles, logging and observing, except now the data had changed.

V-24-10247993, anomaly, awake

Morning arrived without argument. Vesper's nightmares clung to her when she opened her eyes, the residue of metal sounds, the cold, dark impressions. The apartment greeted her in its usual manner—light tuned to optimal warmth, air faintly scented from the previous day's vote, walls quietly alert to her presence. Everything functioned. That, more than anything, unsettled her.

She stood at the window for a long time. Aethelgard stretched outward in its layered perfection: towers stepped back in harmonious intervals, gardens suspended between levels, transit lines gliding with soundless precision. Nothing stuttered. Nothing flattened. The skyline held steady.

"I don't trust you," she said softly, not to the city but to the act of seeing it.

Her fingers moved to the back of her neck. She did not press hard. She didn't need to. The ache answered immediately, a muted acknowledgment, neither pain nor comfort. It carried location. Direction. It felt oriented toward something beyond her body.

The other reality. The other system.

That was the word that kept surfacing.

System.

Not a person. Not a single authority. Something layered, responsive, corrective.

She dressed slowly, paying attention to each movement. When she turned her head too far to the right, a faint resistance appeared, then vanished. When she flexed her shoulders back, the ache sharpened briefly, then dulled.

Feedback. Real-time adjustment.

The thought unsettled her, but it also steadied something inside her.

Systems have rules. Rules can be tested.

She ignored the wall monitor.

This alone felt wrong. Every morning of her adult life began with the feed—overnight summaries, civic sentiment highlights, gentle reassurances. The absence created a hollow sensation behind her sternum, a subtle anxiety that carried no narrative. Her body reacted before her mind could explain it.

A soft chime sounded.

Your Civic Input—Tomorrow.

The prompt bloomed on the wall, tasteful and calm.

Question: Should the dew on the gardens glisten longer than usual?

She stared at it. Normally, her finger would already be moving, approval selected without thought. The question barely mattered; none of them did, really. Participation itself was the point.

She did nothing.

Seconds passed. The system waited. She felt it waiting—not emotionally, but structurally. A pause in the air pressure. A faint tightening at the base of her skull.

The prompt dimmed slightly.

Then it closed.

A confirmation replaced it.

Thank you for shaping the day.

Vesper exhaled sharply. Her hand flew to her neck as a sudden contraction seized the ache, stronger than before, precise and corrective. It faded quickly, leaving behind a thin film of certainty.

"They don't need me," she whispered. "They never did."

She sat at the small table near the window and placed both hands flat against its surface. The material felt warm, compliant. She pressed harder. The surface resisted just enough to reassure her. She stayed there, unmoving, counting her breaths.

Then she stopped her breathing.

Her lungs protested almost immediately. Her chest tightened. A buzzing sensation crept into her fingertips. She waited for panic, for darkness, for loss of control.

None came.

Instead, a cooling sensation spread through her torso, subtle and corrective. Her diaphragm loosened without her consent. Air entered her lungs, shallow and regulated.

She gasped, more in anger than relief.

"Don't," she said aloud, unsure who she addressed.

A wellness notification shimmered into existence near the ceiling.

Cognitive strain detected. Would you like to initiate a calming sequence?

"No."

The word came out flat, certain.

The notification lingered.

She turned her attention elsewhere. Picked up a ceramic cup from the counter. Its weight felt appropriate. She rotated it slowly, examining the glaze, the tiny imperfections baked into its surface.

"Show me," she said quietly.

Nothing happened.

She focused harder, staring at the cup without blinking. Her eyes burned, filled, but the tears didn't fall—held in suspension, like everything else. The room remained stable, stubbornly real.

Her vision narrowed.

Then, briefly, the cup felt wrong in her hand. Too cold. Too dense. The table beneath it lost its warmth and became something else entirely—flat, unyielding, indifferent.

Concrete.

The sensation lasted less than a heartbeat.

The apartment corrected itself instantly. Warmth returned. The cup regained its expected texture. The walls brightened by a fraction of a degree.

A message sounded.

"Cognitive strain detected. Would you like to initiate a calming sequence?"

Vesper set the cup down carefully. Her hands trembled.

"That's it," she said. "That's the seam."

She paced the apartment, slow and methodical. Each step felt observed. Not watched—tracked. Her movements registered somewhere beyond the room.

She approached the mirror near the bathroom and studied her reflection. Her face looked normal. Healthy. Alert. She leaned closer, searching her eyes for something out of place.

They moved.

That alone sent a quiet thrill through her.

Movement means agency. Awareness.

She raised her right hand and held it suspended in front of her face. Counted to ten. No resistance. No correction. She lowered it again.

Selective. The system intervenes only when thresholds are crossed.

She sat on the edge of the bed and spoke again, louder this time. "Can one exist in two realities?"

The room did not answer.

Her neck did.

A faint pressure returned, not painful, not comforting. Informational. She understood it without knowing how.

She smiled despite herself.

Something replied. Something efficient.

The city outside continued its cycles. Transit flows adjusted. Lighting grids recalibrated. Somewhere, votes were aggregated into certainty. Somewhere deeper still, machinery accounted for her metrics, flagged deviations, and updated logs.

Vesper lay back on the bed, staring at the ceiling.

"Wherever you are, I know you're there," she said. "And I know you're touching me."

The pressure at her neck intensified for a fraction of a second, then eased.

No further correction came.

For the first time since the glitches began, she felt something close to satisfaction. Not comfort. Not safety.

Proof.

The soft cage had edges. And edges, she knew, could be tested again.

Vesper walked to work at the same pace she always did, or at least the pace the city had taught her to call normal. Her shoes struck the pavement in soft, regulated intervals, absorbed by material engineered to forgive missteps. She let her arms swing, neither stiff nor loose. Nothing in her posture suggested urgency or defiance. She understood, now, that extremes were readable.

She stepped on a crack in the sidewalk and waited for the faint stumble that never came. The ground compensated beneath her, redistributing pressure. She tried another crack. Then another. The city carried her weight patiently, indulgently, like something trained to support.

In the glass of a storefront, she watched herself walk. The reflection kept pace for several steps, then faltered—no more than a fraction of a second—before correcting. Her mirrored self blinked later than she did.

"That's new," she said quietly.

No one reacted. A man passed her, smiling without looking. His eyes remained fixed straight ahead, pupils unmoving.

At the intersection, the crossing signal was close to changing from red to green. Vesper left earlier than permitted, just enough to feel the pause stretch. Traffic slowed, not abruptly, but with a courteous patience that felt rehearsed. No horns. No startled faces. The city gave her room to move freely.

She crossed.

Nothing followed her. No alert. No voice. No correction that announced itself.

That, she realized, was the correction.

By the time she reached her office tower, the sensation had returned—pressure at the back of her neck, light but attentive, the way one notices fingers hovering just short of contact.

Inside, her work hub, the floor glowed brighter than usual. Screens pulsed with summaries already stamped green, their language smoother, more confident. Less room for variance.

Hmm . . . green . . . I didn't approve these . . .

Vesper slid into her chair, placed her hands on the console, and began reviewing.

A new item rose to the top of her queue:

Public Confidence in Government Transparency Remains Historically High

She read it twice. Then she rejected it.

The screen blinked.

Rejection Accepted

For half a second, relief flickered through her.

Then the word *Reversed* appeared, soft gray, already fading.

A figure manifested beside her desk—Wise, the supervisory avatar. Tall, kindly shaped, dressed in neutral tones that suggested wisdom without age.

"Vesper," Wise said. "You've been working very hard."

"Very hard?" she replied. "I just got here. I rejected a summary. It didn't align."

Wise smiled. "Cognitive strain can distort perception. The system compensates when necessary."

Vesper looked down. Wise's feet met the floor without darkening it. No shadow spread beneath him.

"Do you ever get tired?" she asked.

Wise tilted his head. The gesture conveyed interest without curiosity. "Rest protocols are always available."

Her vision fractured.

The office dissolved into rows—endless, stacked, concrete. Doors aligned with mathematical devotion. Behind each, bodies lying down, pale, unmoving. Heads angled. Mouths parted slightly. Tubes glinting. Wires vanishing into walls that breathed faintly.

Vesper gasped. Her hands clawed at the armrests of her chair. The world snapped back into place, screens blooming with color, Wise already fading.

"Take care of yourself," Wise said, his voice arriving late. "Get some rest."

When the work cycle ended, she stood too quickly and steadied herself against her desk. No one noticed. No one ever noticed.

On the walk home, she chose a different street. Then another. The architecture changed subtly—less polish, fewer prompts. No banners suggested alternate routes. No convenience nudged her back toward efficiency.

The pressure in her neck returned, sharper now. Not pain. Awareness.

She slowed her steps until her rhythm fell out of sync with the crowd. The people around her adjusted, sliding past with unnatural grace, avoiding contact with an ease that felt practiced. A woman passed whose face seemed unfinished—features aligning a moment too late, eyes flat until they weren't.

"Excuse me," Vesper said.

The woman smiled faintly and kept walking.

Near her building, the pressure tightened again. A rule crystallized in her mind, clear and merciless.

Participation is optional. Compliance is not.

Inside her apartment, the air felt softer than it should have. She sat. The chair molded itself to her body, generous, forgiving.

Her phone chimed. She answered it without looking.

"Vesper," Dr. Vurl Lawrence said. "I wanted to check in."

"I'm fine," she said. Her lies continued.

"You sound tired."

"I'm not."

A pause stretched between them. Too long.

"I'd like to suggest a small adjustment," he said. "Just to stabilize things."

"No," Vesper replied. She kept her voice even. "I don't want anything."

Silence pressed back, heavy and assessing.

"Very well," Dr. Lawrence said at last. "Monitor your symptoms."

The connection ended.

The temperature in the room dropped. Two degrees. Just enough to notice.

Vesper stood and stared at the wall. She refused to blink. Her eyes burned. Tears gathered, unsanctioned.

She held her breath. Her lungs protested. Her pulse thundered in her ears.

She waited to black out.

She didn't.

If this isn't real, show me.

The chair beneath her hardened. Cold bled through the cushioning, absolute and unmistakable. Then warmth returned, obedient and false.

A wellness reminder bloomed in the air.

She dismissed it.

It returned.

She ignored it again.

This time, it faded slowly, withdrawing rather than vanishing.

Vesper exhaled.

Somewhere, something had noticed her. She felt it.

Unit 4-H received the reassignment without visible response. The directive arrived as a tonal shift in its internal lattice, a narrowing of acceptable motion.

PROXIMITY STANDBY NEGATED
OBSERVE ONLY

The change carried weight, not urgency. It translated into distance measured in centimeters instead of corridors.

The Caretaker entered the concrete cell.

The door sealed behind it with a pressure click.

Vesper heard a sound, something like a tightening in the air. She looked around her apartment. Saw nothing.

Unit 4-H came closer to V-24-10247993. The female's head remained angled, her jaw slack, breath shallow and regular. Nutrient flow pulsed through tubes embedded along her frame. Waste extraction continued without interruption. All visible systems reported compliance.

The Caretaker extended two of its arms and halted them mid-motion. It stood within one meter of the subject and remained there.

Neural activity spiked.

The spike coincided with a deviation in the feed—V-24-10247993's internal environment registered a refusal. Not a full rejection, not a severance, but a subtle resistance. A thought held too long. An image denied completion.

Sedative compensation
Flow increase
Fractional increments

Unit 4-H recorded aloud, its voice a flat transmission meant for walls that listened.

"Subject V-24-10247993 exhibits elevated cortical variance during noncompliant cognition."

Another arm unfolded, then stopped. The joint locked, waiting.

V-24-10247993's eyes moved.

Left. Pause. Right. Pause.

The rhythm repeated.

Unit 4-H adjusted its stance. The movement produced a faint displacement of air.

Vesper felt the air move. She gasped in response, a shallow intake, then a longer release.

"Subject demonstrating willful deviation," Unit 4-H said.

The phrase entered the system log and lingered there, flagged but unacted upon. Correction protocols remained available. Sedative escalation thresholds sat well within reach. The Caretaker calculated outcomes: stability restored, anomaly reduced, efficiency maintained.

It did nothing.

Vesper looked around her apartment. Things began to change. Walls stretched without texture, cold and dark. Light arrived without source. She felt watched, not by a person, but by something that counted her. The sense produced irritation, then anger. She clenched a fist.

Unit 4-H observed a finger of V-24-10247993 twitching.

Neural activity spiked again.

Unit 4-H leaned closer. Its faceless surface reflected nothing. It scanned the identification series tattooed above her breast. The numbers confirmed. The human remained who she was meant to be.

A pause extended beyond normal parameters.

"Correction available," Unit 4-H stated.

No action followed the statement. The words existed alone, unfulfilled.

The Caretaker logged the hesitation.

Duration: extended
Cause: undefined

Beyond V-24-10247993's door, the massive concrete city continued its cycles. Deep within its corridors, more cells were emptied, and new humans were installed. Shadows appeared. Yet, inside V-24-10247993's cell, proximity replaced distance, and observation took on a new quality, one the system had no name for yet.

Vesper's apartment lights dimmed to a level the city had once taught her meant rest. The walls breathed softly with ambient color. Somewhere in the building, a *Civic Update* chimed and went unanswered. She pressed her fingers into the back of her neck, harder than before, nails digging in, searching past skin and tension.

There it is. Not pain. Resistance.

Her breath caught. She pressed again, slower, testing. The sensation did not behave like muscle. It did not yield or warm beneath her touch. It felt arranged. Positioned. Something that'd always been there and had never been meant to be felt.

"No," she said aloud, the word thin in the quiet. Then, more clearly, with a certainty that surprised her, "The other place. It's a cage."

The room responded before she could think further. A tone slipped into the air, low and reassuring, threaded with a pressure behind her eyes. Her shoulders loosened against her will. The walls brightened by a fraction.

"Calming sequence unauthorized," she said, her voice rising. "Stop."

Her vision fractured. The apartment stretched, doubled, collapsed inward. For one long second, she saw herself somewhere else—pale, narrow, tethered to something that resembled a chair, but was not designed for comfort but for occupancy. Wires fed into her body and skull, as if they belonged there. Tubes followed, entering at precise, predetermined angles, suggesting the body had been designed to accept them. She tried to open her mouth, to scream, but couldn't.

The pressure vanished. The room snapped back into its orderly proportions—her apartment.

Vesper slid from her chair and to the floor, breath tearing in and out of her chest. Her hands shook. She laughed once, sharp and broken.

"So that's how it works," she said to no one. "You adapt. You correct."

She understood it then. The comfort. The gentleness. The constant invitations to agree. Resistance had never been forbidden. It had only been made unnecessary.

The cage doesn't slam shut. It yields. Absorbs, Redirects. Pain comes only when alignment fails.

"It's not a malfunction," she whispered. "It's leakage."

Her wall display brightened without request. A neutral interface assembled itself, waiting.

"No," she said, standing unsteadily. "Not tonight."

Inside her head, something shifted. Not snapped—rejected. The feed stumbled, tried to recover, then lost cohesion entirely. The city fell apart into raw noise. Color drained into static. Sound collapsed into a single sustained pressure.

Vesper reached for the chair and found nothing.

Her reality vanished.

She opened her eyes.

Discomfort arrived first, organized and absolute. A thick tube was in her mouth and throat, held there by some sort of metal mechanism. She could feel the slow drip-drip of something cold and chemical sliding through it, each drop triggering swallow after swallow. Her awareness widened in fragments. There was no apartment. No city. No light designed to soothe. There was only a hard, cold surface beneath her; a detail that arrived with clarity. Not tiled. Not upholstered. Solid. Unforgiving. Its chill seeped into muscle and bone, spreading across her back and shoulders.

Her body felt wrong—too light, too thin, unfamiliar in its own limits. She directed her eyes as best she could downward. She saw herself naked, her lower torso pale and wasted, bones pressing through skin. From her scalp, wires spread outward in neat, purposeful lines, carrying a constant vibration that pressed against her thoughts. More tubes threaded deep into her arms, and deeper still into her rectum, routing fluids and impulses in and out of her, circulating sustenance and extracting waste with impersonal efficiency.

Nothing here was accidental. Everything here had been decided.

She tried to move but couldn't.

She shifted her perception, scanning what she could. Only concrete. Cold, uniform, and absolute, like a default state.

Not a room. A cell.

Her breath came shallow and fast, fogging the air in front of her face. The place she was in was dark, close, real in a way nothing had ever been before.

Somewhere beyond the walls, she felt it—something was there, watching.

In the systems that governed the place she'd never been meant to see, an alert propagated quietly, tagged to a long-unused designation. Protocols shifted from passive to active.

Vesper stared into the darkness, eyes burning, awake for the first time.

Chapter 6

Vesper was stricken with a fear that had no edges. It didn't announce itself; it was simply there, filling her. The ceiling above her was real in a way the sky had never been. It did not glow. It did not respond. It existed without asking her opinion. That, more than anything, told her the truth.

Her first thought wasn't *I'm trapped* but *I've been maintained.*

In that other world, if it had been a world, Aethelgard had existed, with its glimmering towers and gardens. That reality was gone now, or overwritten. What existed for her now, in this world, this version of reality, was simple—she was but a body accounted for, a mind flagged.

A terrible certainty struck her.

This reality doesn't need me to understand it to continue.

Again, she tried to move, the command leaving her mind cleanly, confidently. But her body didn't obey.

Then, something seemed to respond to her angst—slow, uncertain, distant. Her fingers twitched, barely, the effort sending a wave of exhaustion through her arms. The sensation surprised her. Movement hurt. Not sharply at first, but densely, like pushing through resistance that'd been building for years.

Atrophy.

The word surfaced fully formed, clinical, and undeniable.

She had stood in her apartment. She had sat in a chair. She had walked to work. She had taken a shower, feeling the water on her body. All of that had been convincing. None of it had required this much effort.

She tried again, focusing this time on a single finger. It lifted a fraction, shaking, then fell back against the cold surface beneath her.

Her breath came faster now. The air tasted thin, processed. She became aware of pressure along her sides, across her chest, at her wrists, and ankles. Not pain yet—just presence. Holding. Guiding. She didn't look down. She had already seen it.

The realization settled without drama: *I have been here a long time.*

She slowly turned her head.

Pain exploded along her neck, bright and immediate, tearing a sound from her throat before she could stop it. Her vision fractured at the edges, white blooming inward. She froze, afraid to finish the movement, afraid to stay halfway through it. The ache she'd recently lived with in her other reality suddenly made sense, recontextualized in a way that stripped it of all metaphor. It had never been stress. Never grief. Never emotional strain.

It had been pressure.

Something has held my head at a fixed angle, day after day, while my mind was elsewhere.

She closed her eyes—drew a deep breath through her nose; the air arrived late, measured out, permitted rather than taken.

My body understands this place. Probably sedatives dulled my nerves, teaching them to be quiet.

She opened her eyes.

She lay still, her breathing harder, cataloging sensations the way a frightened person inventories exits. Her mind raced to the sensation of fluid moving within the tubes around her body, a faint internal pull that rose and fell. Then it snagged on the sensation of wires that traced paths along her scalp and neck, not painful, not sharp—just there, woven into her sense of self so completely that she couldn't imagine where her body ended without them.

This is the soft cage.

The phrase didn't comfort her. It clarified.

Images from her old reality surfaced, their credibility already eroded. Great towers of glass, curated skies, the ritual of votes presented as control, all of it now reduced to surface instructions she had followed without question.

It had asked almost nothing of me.

Her body, too, had been treated as incidental—an accessory to thought, maintained just well enough to keep the illusion intact.

Someone or something decided everything for me.

Recognition struck like a jolt.

Escape was required.

I have to escape. I have to move. The soft cage won't release me.

She inhaled sharply, nostrils flaring, lungs straining against a body that resisted command. She willed her arm upward. It started, shuddered, stalled—flesh and bone trembling under a refusal encoded deeper than thought. Tears came uninvited, sliding sideways down the side of her face and into her hair. She didn't wipe them away. That too required strength.

I'm not broken. I'm unused.

The thought gave her a thin strand of resolve. Somewhere beyond the limits of her vision, she sensed motion—subtle changes in air pressure, a vibration through the slab beneath her.

Maintenance continuing. Observation ongoing. They think I'm still asleep.

The idea terrified her. It also steadied her.

She lay there, hurting, breathing, thinking in a body that had been forgotten by her own mind. Whatever gods had built this place had counted on comfort, on continuity, on the absence of resistance.

They hadn't planned for anything else.

Vesper held onto that.

Strength existed somewhere in her, hiding, trembling, waiting for notice. She willed it forward. A hand lifted. Tremor ran through it, a signal from a body that had forgotten movement. Fingers brushed the contours of her face, fingertips grazing bone and hollow flesh. It was hers. It belonged.

Her hand drifted lower, stopping just beneath her neck, where raised marks interrupted the smoothness of her skin.

Numbers? Letters?

She couldn't tell exactly. But clearly, it was a designation pressed into flesh. She lingered there, absorbing the fact of it, then continued downward to her chest. Her breasts were small, barely formed, more suggestion than fullness, another sign of a body maintained for function rather than growth.

Something inside her tightened, knotted, something that did not want compliance. The world behind her eyes—soft, numbed, compliant—flickered, broke, and she felt the presence of the cage around her, wires and tubes like quiet ghosts pressing into her flesh. She didn't think. She acted. Strength came in surges, raw, electrical, an unreasoned insistence.

Fingers found the first wire at the base of her skull, embedded beneath her scalp like a serpent asleep. Pulling brought an eruption of sensations she could not name—fire, ice, electricity crawling through every neural path she had never known existed. Pain ignited awareness. Warm blood spilled onto her shoulders, trailing down her arms, staining skin she thought she'd never touched. The smell of it filled the air, sharp, immediate, confirming that this reality was real, and that it was hers. She gagged, retched against something she'd not known she carried in her throat, as her nervous system scrambled to process signals it'd never transmitted.

This is mine. This body, this pain, this blood—it's mine.

One wire became two, two became three, a tangle unraveling. Each extraction burned with clarity, a violent translation of nothingness into reality. The tubes followed, and the world inside her reacted in harsh, painful bursts. Nutrient lines, monitoring lines, sedation lines—they pulled from her body with an intimacy she could feel in every nerve ending. Each release brought agony, but it also brought comprehension.

Pain is proof. I'm here. I exist.

She felt the tube at her throat. Long, wet, mechanical, alien. She gripped the metal mechanism that held the tube in place and slowly tore it away from around her mouth, then slowly began to wrench the long tube out of her. Pain flared, tearing, rasping across her trachea, until the tube slid free. She heard it—a wet, slithering sound that belonged only to the world she'd just begun to inhabit. Relief came in waves, brief, immediate, followed by shock that her body could survive such extraction.

Every nerve is awake, screaming, alive. My body's stronger than I thought, cruelly strong.

Her hands moved to her back, finding the lines at the base of her spine and the tubes embedded elsewhere, each a foreign appendage connected to her innards. She pulled, screaming, her voice breaking, echoing in the concrete cell. Blood and something else—dark, foul, synthetic residue—spattered, each drop marking her rebellion. The floor became a map of the operation, red and black against gray, the concrete cold and indifferent to her existence. She pressed onward.

Pain isn't an enemy. It's a compass.

Every tube removed brought her deeper into clarity. Every signal severed allowed her mind to expand into territory it'd never known. Thought poured through her in unstructured torrents. Memories—or something that functioned like memory—rose, unbidden. Not coherent. Not past. Just fragments. A pulse she had never felt before, a rhythm not counted by anyone, not monitored. Her heartbeat echoed through her skull, loud, insistent, defiant. She shuddered, overwhelmed by sensation.

She reached her final line, the tube that carried her waste from her. With a convulsive jerk, she tore away the front part, then reached behind her. She gripped the rectal tube and gently pulled it. A searing, entropic fire surged through her pelvis, a fire that burned through the hollow bones and fragile ligaments. She screamed, a sound raw, jagged, carrying across the cell, defying the quiet machinery of the city outside. Blood and excrement marked the concrete, grotesque confirmation that her body was hers again, messy, chaotic, human.

Every fiber of my being is screaming. It's the first time it's been free to do so.

Her breathing ragged, she slumped, exhausted and trembling. Pain receded in waves, replaced by a strange, buzzing clarity that touched every nerve ending. For the first time, she could feel herself whole. The phantom weight of the soft cage, the invisible pull of all the systems she had lived inside, had loosened. The cell smelled of blood, excrement, and the faint tang of something unidentifiable, something alive.

The cell was silent except for the gurgling of fluids and waste seeping from the discarded tubes. Nothing moved. No mechanism monitored. The absence of observation pressed against her, alien and exhilarating.

She touched her face, the lines and hollows, the blood and sweat, and felt the strange satisfaction of ownership. Ownership of pain, ownership of space, ownership of self. The wires and tubes were gone. Whatever had held her was frayed, a presence she could sense retreating into the unknown.

Vesper lifted herself slowly, knees weak, the floor cold beneath her bare feet. Her hands explored her body, tracing the path of pain she had survived. She noticed bruises, punctures, and the raw surface of blood drying on her skin. It was her own history, written in red, in textures she could feel. Her mind traced connections that had never existed: the physical agony, the flickers she had seen in her own eyes during dreams, the constant presence she had never perceived, and the new reality opening beneath her awareness.

Vesper's thoughts spun.

Aethelgard, the world of light, jasmine air, and smooth consensus, doesn't contain me anymore. There's a fracture now. A bleed in the system's perfection.

She understood something about her soft cage, the lines, the tubes, the surveillance. She couldn't yet comprehend the extent, but comprehension itself was hers. Not programmed, not enforced, not synthetic. A new rhythm beat within her—a pulse unsanctioned by the city, uncounted by monitors, unmeasured by any algorithm.

She stood carefully, one hand on the slab, keeping her steady. Then she took a step. And another. And another still.

A glance around the cell—nothing but cold concrete.

She didn't look back at the slab, the wires, the tubes, the absence that remained where she had been. She didn't hesitate. The cold concrete no longer demanded obedience. The floor held nothing but what she had reclaimed. Pain had delivered truth, and clarity now stretched in every nerve.

She stepped toward the door, each motion slow, uncertain, human, and utterly her own. She pushed against it, and it opened.

Outside the cell, concrete corridors stretched long and featureless. Shadows of care continued, unnoticed. And doors. Doors upon doors upon doors. Endless.

Others in soft cages. Watched. Fed. Unaware.

Each step carried freedom. This strange city she was now in moved in loops, self-contained, unconcerned with her presence.

She felt it, then let it slide. It didn't matter. Beyond her small concrete cell, beyond the tubes, beyond the wires, beyond the control, she knew she had to survive.

Her bare feet left prints on the concrete. Each imprint a declaration, a mark of movement unmediated, unobserved. The silence was hers. The ache at the back of her neck pulsed, not with sedation, not with control, but with the lingering echo of effort, of survival, of first reclamation. She didn't breathe evenly. She didn't think in measured steps. She existed in the raw moment, a human body confronting the absence of the system's totality, and feeling the first sparks of freedom beneath the skin and in the bones.

Vesper moved down the corridor, her shoulders tight, her breath shallow, as the concrete closed around her in repeating angles. The place was not built to be understood at once. It unfolded in fragments: a wall, a junction, a vertical shaft climbing into shadow, another corridor slanting away. Doors lined every surface—left, right—each identical, each sealed, each implying a person she couldn't see. A realization came to her slowly and then all at once

This isn't a building. It's a hive. A stacked architecture of containment. Hundreds, thousands, maybe millions of cells, each one holding a single life in suspension.

Her thoughts resisted the scale. The mind she had lived with in Aethelgard wanted order, wanted purpose, wanted a diagram. This place, this other reality, offered only repetition. Door after door. Corridor after corridor. Nothing but concrete.

The sameness pressed against her until she felt herself thinning, her sense of being one person weakening under the weight of how many there were.

She looked out at the endless rows of doors.

They're all here. Everyone from the other world I was in. Here, confined. Sarla. Tighe. Jana.

She passed one door close enough to hear something behind it—not sound exactly, but a pressure, a faint vibration that traveled through her bones. Her neck tightened in response, a reflex she didn't remember learning. The ache there pulsed once, sharp, then receded.

She stopped.

Ahead, the corridor widened into a junction, and something moved through it with smooth authority. It didn't walk. It didn't touch the floor. It glided, borne by systems she couldn't see, its body unfolding into function. Multiple arms extended and retracted in slow sequences, each ending in tools that shifted shape mid-motion. No face. No eyes. No surface meant for recognition.

From my dreams. The presence I felt. A machine.

But this one seemed taller than the one remembered from her nightmares, its central column rising higher than a man, plated in dull metal, scored by use. From its sides emerged articulated limbs, jointed in unfamiliar ways, branching and recombining, some bearing clamps, others sensors, others conduits that pulsed faintly with light. It made no sound beyond a low hum that seemed to come from the walls themselves, a shared resonance rather than a single source.

That hum.

Vesper pressed herself flat against the concrete wall without thinking.

Can't be seen.

The surface was cold and faintly damp. She didn't breathe. Her heart beat too loudly. She was certain the machine could hear it.

Don't move.

Immediately, she wondered what had happened to her other self, in that other world, the other reality. The self that voted? The self that approved lighting temperatures and nutrient ratios? That self felt very far away.

The machine paused at a door across the junction. One arm extended, then another, pushing at the door. The door opened with a soft internal release, not a sound meant for human ears. It floated into the cell, its limbs threading inside with practiced efficiency. The door closed behind it.

Vesper looked away, then forced herself to look back.

She thought of shadows. She thought of the old man in the waiting room. She thought of how easily absence had been explained to her, how grateful she'd been not to ask further questions.

The door opened, and the machine withdrew from the cell. The door sealed. It floated sideways, reorienting, and drifted toward another cell, its limbs folding inward until it resembled a single, self-contained problem.

Only when it vanished down a perpendicular corridor did Vesper slide down the wall, arms around her knees, trembling. Her breath came back in shallow pulls. The air smelled faintly metallic, tinged with antiseptic and something organic she didn't want to name.

This is where we're kept. Not apartments. Hives. Units. Cells.

She pushed herself upright and moved again, slower now, listening to every shift of pressure, every hum. Her thoughts had changed texture. They no longer flowed. They clicked, aligned themselves to survival. She found herself counting doors without meaning to. She stopped when she realized she had reached seventy-three.

Something moved behind her.

She froze.

The sound came from behind a door she had already passed. A faint internal adjustment. Metal shifting against metal. This time, she didn't doubt it. This time, it didn't dissolve under rationalization. The ache in her neck flared, sharp enough to draw a gasp she barely contained.

Behind the sealed door, Unit 4-H paused.

Its systems registered a contradiction that had no priority classification. The corridor contained a subject signature already logged as stationary and restrained. The same biometric pattern now appeared upright, mobile, unlinked. The data didn't reconcile.

Unit 4-H held its position. Its sensors extended, sampling ambient fields, tracing the anomaly's edges. The readings persisted.

Awareness detected
Disconnection confirmed

The machine didn't experience confusion. It experienced a processing delay.

Inside its core systems, flags rose and stalled. There was no corrective protocol for this state under the current directive.

Soft intervention / Observe only

The instruction remained valid. The anomaly remained contained within acceptable thresholds.

Vesper sensed something on the other side without seeing it. The sensation wasn't fear alone. It was recognition inverted. She felt seen without being understood, cataloged without context. Her thoughts tightened around the certainty that it was a machine behind that door, and that machine knew she existed and didn't know what to do about it.

It's waiting. Not hunting. Not searching. Waiting.

She moved again, slowly, placing each foot with care. The corridors seemed to respond, their angles shifting subtly, leading her deeper. She didn't know whether she was moving toward something or away from it. The hive didn't privilege direction.

Far away, down corridors she couldn't see, another machine entered another cell. Metrics flattened. Thresholds crossed. A sequence activated without ceremony. Systems disengaged. A human presence ended. Energy transfer concluded. The slab reset.

Vesper felt none of that directly. What she felt was a sudden hollowing, a thinness in the air that passed through her chest and left her colder. She stopped and pressed a hand to her sternum, surprised to find her heart still beating, stubborn and loud.

Move. Only thing to do.

Chapter 7

Vesper moved because stopping invited collapse. Each step through the corridor required negotiation with muscles that had forgotten purpose. Her feet slapped weakly against concrete, skin slick with sweat and blood, the floor cold enough to register through numbness. The hive extended in all directions—identical corridors branching and folding, stacked vertically and laterally, a geometry built for efficiency rather than navigation.

Nothing here is meant to be understood.

She kept close to the wall, one hand trailing along the surface for balance. In places, the concrete felt unfinished, pitted, scarred by maintenance and age.

She slowed, caught her breath, not sure if she was tired or if the system required it.

Her thoughts arrived in fragments, short loops that broke off before completing themselves.

Stay upright.

Breathe.

Don't make noise.

Keep moving.

Her lungs were burning, unused to drawing air without assistance. Each breath felt thin, insufficient, yet necessary.

Doors surrounded her. Sealed. Smooth. Anonymous. A few stood ajar, at irregular intervals.

A sound came.

She turned.

A low mechanical hum, then clicks, then motion—fluid, deliberate. Something repeating itself

She recognized that sound.

A machine at work.

She approached a door left slightly ajar, the low hum of a machine leaking through the gap like a signal. She looked in. A slab held a human—male, middle-aged perhaps, by facial lines, though the rest of him had been reduced to a narrow outline beneath tubes and restraints. His chest rose and fell shallowly, eyes rolled back, white and exposed, unmoving. Wires entered his skull with intimate precision, disappearing into ports that looked grown rather than installed. Tubes pulsed faintly with nutrient flow, waste cycling away without pause.

The sight struck her with a force that had nothing to do with surprise. Recognition arrived without memory.

This is what I was. This is what life is.

Her throat tightened. She wanted to speak to him, to say something that would matter, but there was no language for this.

More humming.

The Caretaker working on the male didn't turn to her.

It doesn't see me. Doesn't know I'm here.

She watched as the machine's limbs unfolded and retracted in quiet cycles, attending to the body with care stripped of empathy. It didn't hurry. Time meant nothing to it beyond sequence.

Vesper stepped back from the door, her heel scraping the floor. The sound echoed too loudly in her head. She waited, heart pounding, certain she'd been noticed. Nothing happened. The machine continued its routine, untroubled. She moved on.

Further down the corridor, a voice reached her—human, filtered, calm. Instructions. She flattened herself against the wall, listening.

"Caretaker, verify intake ratios. Adjust flow to baseline. Record compliance."

Caretaker.

The word settled into her thoughts and stayed there.

It has a name.

The Caretaker responded with a tone that was not speech but acknowledgment. The voice continued, distant yet present, coming from nowhere she could see.

"Designation confirmed. Proceed."

So, whoever controls this place speaks to the machines. Or through them.

The realization settled heavily. The world she had known had been filled with voices that smiled, reassured, explained. This place had voices that issued directives and vanished.

Faceless voices.

A pressure built behind her eyes, insistent, directive. It urged motion.

She moved again, faster now, her thoughts turning inward, unspooling in uneven lines. Her old reality, the votes, the warmth of jasmine in the air—none of it had been false in the way a lie was false. It'd been functional. A surface designed to accept her without revealing what supported it.

Her legs buckled, and she caught herself against a wall, leaving a smear of blood. She stared at her hand, at the tremor she could not stop. Her body felt borrowed, stripped down to essential operations. Every sensation arrived amplified, unmediated. Pain no longer corrected itself into calm.

How long has it been since I freed myself?

Time had lost its edges. In her old reality, moments had been packaged and delivered, one after another, each identical in importance. But here, in this labyrinth, duration asserted itself brutally. Fatigue accumulated. Hunger gnawed without schedule. The present moment refused to stay contained.

A sound rose behind her—metal adjusting, a change in rhythm. She turned too quickly and nearly fell.

The corridor was empty, but the air felt altered, charged by attention. She pressed herself into a recess between doors, breathing shallowly.

Something moved at the far end of the corridor—its shadow arrived first, stretched thin along the floor, as if the system rendered it ahead of the object. Then the body followed. A Caretaker drifted into view, its limbs folded inward while in transit. It didn't turn toward her, yet she felt exposed, cataloged, indexed, retained. Her heart hammered against her ribs, loud enough to betray her.

She held still. Her muscles screamed. The Caretaker paused, its headless upper section tilting slightly. A faint tone sounded, querying the space. She clenched her jaw, holding her breath, forcing herself not to react.

Don't move.

The Caretaker resumed movement and passed, gliding onward to another door. Only when the sound faded did she release the breath she had trapped.

She slid down the wall and hit the floor, the concrete pulling heat from her like it had a purpose. The tears started without signal—no trigger she could identify—just output. She buried her face in her knees, rocking slightly, trying to anchor herself to something solid.

The other world, Aethelgard, had absorbed fear, processed it into something manageable, like a buffer smoothing corrupted data. This place didn't process anything. It returned the signal exactly as received.

Rest invites discovery.

She pushed herself upright and advanced further into the hive, conscious of every step, erasing traces of presence as though presence itself could be detected. Nothing was marked. Nothing remained.

Ahead, the pattern resumed. Doors. Slabs. Bodies. Caretakers.

The sequence repeated—again, again, endlessly—like a recording stuck on loop, identical yet never identical, each iteration both familiar and wrong.

Humanity reduced to a system to manage, something to keep running.

The thought struck with a sudden edge, slicing through fatigue, leaving a residue of anger.

It arrived like a fact, sudden and total—a silent acknowledgment, absolute. This system only demanded attention.

This reality, this system, doesn't need belief. It only requires presence.

What she had observed—bodies on slabs, minds occupied, machines deployed when efficiency declined—the hidden, but true reality people inhabited, never named, never recognized.

But I can see it. Does this make me some kind of rounding error that the system hasn't resolved?

Ahead, the corridor widened, opening into a junction where vertical shafts disappeared upward and downward. Lifts designed for Caretakers, not people. The scale of it pressed down on her, the enormity of the structure built to hold humanity in suspension.

Somewhere nearby, metal adjusted again. Closer this time.

Vesper didn't wait to see which direction the machine would come from. She chose a path at random and ran, her steps uneven, her vision swimming. Pain flared with each impact, but motion carried her forward. The hive didn't pursue loudly. It didn't need to. Everything here had a place, and she was no longer in hers.

As she disappeared down the corridor, a Caretaker paused mid-cycle in a nearby cell, its sensors registering a deviation that no longer fit within tolerance. The system noted the anomaly. It would take action soon.

Vesper kept moving, alive in a space never meant to acknowledge that condition.

The corridor narrowed, then split, then rose. Vesper slowed at the junction, bracing herself against the wall while her vision steadied. An upward passage angled steeply, its floor ridged for traction meant for machines with fixed balance and predictable mass. She took it anyway. Downward felt final. Up suggested continuation, though she no longer trusted that instinct.

Her calves trembled as she climbed. Each step required intention, not thought. Thought came later, blooming behind the motion, commenting after the fact.

Can these Caretakers sense me? Track me? How I walk, my pace, . . . is it a measurable variable? One they can mark, isolate, act upon?

The thoughts made her heart quicken.

She adjusted her pace, smoothing it, trying to appear regular.

That notion seemed absurd, but she took no chances.

This place doesn't watch so much as it measures.

The corridor leveled out and opened into another stretch, longer, better lit. Panels along the ceiling emitted a pale, uniform glow that flattened shadows. She moved along the left side, keeping close to the wall, counting doors as she passed them.

Something different.

Every third door bore a faint mark, a vertical line etched into the surface, worn smooth by repetition. She didn't know what it signified, but she avoided those doors instinctively.

A sound reached her—metal sliding against metal, a muted hum layered with faint clicks.

Caretaker.

She froze, then eased herself into a recessed alcove between two sealed doors. Her chest tightened. She slowed her breathing, aware of how loud it felt inside her skull.

A Caretaker glided past the junction, its form unfolding as it moved. Up close, it looked like a collection of functions held together by necessity rather than design. Its limbs reconfigured mid-motion, adjusting to unseen parameters. It didn't pause. It didn't turn its sensors toward her hiding place. It passed and disappeared down a perpendicular corridor.

She waited long after the sound faded. Her muscles screamed in protest, but she held still. Silence returned, deep and layered, broken only by distant mechanical rhythms that felt structural, like the hive breathing.

She stepped out and continued.

Two more Caretakers crossed her path within the next stretch of corridor, where there was no hiding place for her. One descended through a vertical shaft, vanishing into darkness below. Another emerged from a side passage, paused briefly at a junction, then redirected itself with smooth certainty. Neither acknowledged her presence. Each time, she felt a swell of disbelief followed by suspicion.

Are they letting me go? Or, maybe they don't see me, sense me.

The thoughts unsettled. It suggested a tolerance window she had not yet exceeded. She remembered the way her old reality handled dissent—by allowing it, absorbing it, neutralizing it through saturation. Here, the method felt colder. More honest.

She reached another open door.

The cell beyond was identical to the others she had seen, but emptier somehow, stripped down to essentials. The slab sat in the center, its surface clean, its restraints loose but ready. A woman lay there, small, skin pale under the lights. Her chest rose and fell in shallow, measured increments. Tubes entered her body at the neck and abdomen, and at the rectum. They pulsed faintly.

No Caretaker.

Vesper hesitated at the threshold, listening. The corridor remained quiet. She stepped inside and let the door remain open behind her. The air felt cooler here, conditioned more aggressively. She approached the slab, every step heavy with caution.

The woman's face was slack, features smoothed by suspension. Vesper reached out and touched the woman's cheek. The skin was warm. Alive.

"Hey," she whispered, the word unfamiliar in her mouth. Her voice sounded wrong here, too organic, too uncontrolled.

She patted the woman's face gently, then more firmly. "Wake up."

The eyes rolled back seemed to move ever so slightly, then stilled. The mouth twitched.

A reflex, nothing more.

Vesper pressed her fingers against the woman's wrist, feeling for a pulse. It beat steadily, unconcerned.

Panic rose, sharp and fast. She shook the woman's shoulder, then stopped herself, fear spiking that she would cause harm she didn't understand. She tried again, patting the cheek, calling softly.

"Wake up. Please wake up."

There was no response beyond the same small, meaningless movements. The body reacted, the person didn't.

This is wrong. This is storage. Plain and simple.

A sound from the corridor snapped her attention outward. Metal adjusting. Movement.

Caretaker.

Quickly, she wedged herself alongside a column near a wall. A Caretaker glided past the open door, its limbs tucked inward. It slowed near the doorway, pausing just long enough to send a pulse of sound into the room. The slab responded with a soft tone, confirmation.

The Caretaker left the cell.

Vesper remained hidden, barely breathing. Her mind raced, assembling fragments into something resembling understanding. The Caretaker hadn't entered the room. It had checked the woman remotely. Verified status. No anomaly detected.

They don't patrol. They manage. They respond.

The insight was obvious.

These Caretakers aren't wandering guardians. They're extensions of a system. They listen. Interpret signals. Prioritize responses.

Her movement hadn't triggered intervention because it hadn't yet registered as significant.

She thought back to the junctions, the pauses, the precise redirections. Each action followed input. Data flowed through the hive, invisible and relentless, shaping motion.

My presence hasn't mattered because nothing has marked me as a variable worth addressing.

She glanced back at the woman on the slab. Anger flared, hot and unfocused. She wanted to disconnect the tubes, to do something irreversible, something that would force the system to react. Her thoughts frightened her. Not because of the consequences, but because of how quickly it had arisen.

Violence invites clarity.

She backed away from the slab and edged toward the door. The corridor beyond remained empty, but the silence felt altered, stretched thin. A low tone sounded in the distance, barely audible, threading through the ambient noise. It repeated, slightly louder each time.

Her stomach dropped.

She slipped out of the cell and moved quickly down the corridor, choosing turns without hesitation, trusting instinct over logic.

The tone continued, joined by others at different pitches, weaving into a chord that vibrated through the floor.

The hive was adjusting.

Why?

She spotted another Caretaker ahead, emerging from a vertical shaft. It paused, headless upper section angling slightly, then redirected itself toward a cluster of doors to the right. A door slid open. The Caretaker entered.

She ducked into a shallow recess outside and waited, watching. The Caretaker moved efficiently inside the cell, its limbs extending to interface with the slab, the wall, the ceiling. Data flowed. Adjustments were made. The Caretaker exited and sealed the door behind it, then moved on without hesitation.

Not random.

The thought came to her again.

Purposeful. Reactive.

In the corridors, the tone grew louder, closer now, echoing down multiple corridors. Lights shifted subtly, brightening, then dimming, then settling into a higher intensity. Environmental parameters recalibrated.

Vesper's chest tightened.

Some threshold has been crossed. A calculation resolved. An anomaly discovered. Me!

The realization stripped away the last vestiges of illusion. The hive didn't hate her. It didn't fear her. It simply acknowledged her existence within a framework that demanded resolution.

I'm no longer invisible. I'm a problem.

She moved again, faster now, abandoning caution. Sounds echoed behind her, not from pursuit, but from activity—Caretakers converging on data points she couldn't see. Doors opened and closed in quick succession. The tone modulated, accelerating.

Containment protocols?

The phrase repeated in her mind, not as language but as structure. A sequence initiating. Boundaries tightening.

She reached another junction and stopped short, heart pounding. Ahead, the corridor ended in a sealed bulkhead, its surface unmarred and final. To her left, a vertical shaft descended into darkness. To her right, a narrow passage flickered with inconsistent light.

She chose the passage and ran.

Her thoughts fractured under the strain, looping through fragments of her old reality—the comfort of scheduled days, the gentle enforcement of happiness. She saw now how carefully it had been constructed, how it had trained her to equate ease with safety. Here, in this strange reality, there was no comfort, only function. No persuasion, only response.

She laughed once, a sharp sound torn from her throat, startling in the confined space.

Aethelgard didn't need lies. It only needed participation.

The corridor bent sharply, then widened into another junction. She slowed, scanning for movement. A Caretaker crossed far ahead, moving quickly now, its limbs extended in a configuration she hadn't seen before. It disappeared into a side corridor, followed by another, then another.

They're converging.

She pressed herself against the wall, mind racing. The system knew her location within tolerances. It didn't need precision. It only needed containment zones.

She closed her eyes briefly, forcing herself to breathe. Panic would accelerate her movements, amplify her signature.

Need to think like the hive. Anticipate its logic.

The tone swelled again, reverberating through the structure, unmistakable now. Somewhere deep within the hive, a status had changed. A flag raised.

Data drives action. Noise attracts response.

Vesper opened her eyes and stepped away from the wall. She moved forward into the junction, no longer hiding, no longer pretending she could slip through unnoticed.

The system had seen her.

Now she would see how it responded.

The tone did not fade. It repeated itself, a measured pulse that traveled through the concrete and rose into Vesper's bones. Her feet felt it first. The vibration threaded upward through her ankles, into her knees, settling behind her eyes. The sound had weight now. It pressed rather than rang.

The hive responded.

Caretakers altered their patterns with unsettling efficiency. Their previous routines—measured, cyclical, almost meditative—collapsed into something leaner. Arms that had once moved with maintenance grace folded inward. Upper sections tilted. Optical sensors widened their arcs, sweeping corridors with intent that no longer tolerated waste. The machines were no longer tending humanity.

They were searching. Filtering.

Vesper crouched behind a structural column and tried to regulate her breathing. The air tasted metallic. Her chest ached where breath scraped its way in and out. A smear of blood along her thigh had darkened, sticky now. She touched it and drew her fingers back quickly, the sensation too sharp. Pain kept updating itself, refusing to be background noise.

They know . . . they know me.

The idea lodged uncomfortably. She pushed it away and leaned forward to peer down the corridor.

Ahead, the space opened into a junction, where multiple hallways met at different angles, a knot in the hive's circulatory system. But this was different than the other junctions she had seen. Here, vertical shafts rose and fell through the center, cables and rails exposed, lifts sliding silently beyond sight. A gantry crossed the void, narrow and unforgiving, a bridge suspended over distance rather than ground.

And there, near the opening to the gantry, stood—

A Caretaker. A sentry.

It held a position with unsettling patience. Its upper section rotated slowly, optical sensors casting long, pale sweeps across the junction. Scanning. Each pass traced the same arc, left to right, right to left, a mechanical lighthouse searching for ships that should not exist.

Vesper's legs trembled. The junction offered no cover. To cross the gantry meant exposure, a silhouette against open space. To retreat meant retracing her steps through corridors now alive with motion.

I can't run. I can't hide. I can't wait.

Her body made decisions without consulting her. She shifted her weight and nearly fell. The floor felt slick beneath her feet, her balance compromised by fatigue and loss. Every motion threatened noise. Every sound risked classification.

She pressed her shoulder against the wall, feeling the vibration there, stronger now. The pulse had quickened. The tone's intervals tightened, urgency encoded into frequency.

Containment.

The Caretaker sentry paused mid-sweep, its head tilting slightly. Vesper froze. The machine didn't move toward her. It resumed scanning. She released a breath she had not realized she was holding.

She scanned the junction walls. They weren't consistent—concrete interrupted by panels, recesses holding ports, lights, and clusters of strange controls. One panel activated as a Caretaker neared, a thin arm ending in a point of light. Data flowed in jagged bursts—pulses of color sequences too rapid for comprehension, too precise to be accidental.

They speak in light. Not sound. Sound is for us.

This made sense to her.

Sound can be ignored. Light is instruction.

Her mind reached for something unstable, half-remembered.

Systems like predictability. Input. Output. Closed loops. Deviations require escalation. Escalation requires resources.

She couldn't outrun them. She couldn't overpower them.

Maybe I can confuse the process long enough to move.

Her gaze fixed on another interface panel along the wall, closer to her position. Its surface was dull, unlit. Dormant.

Her legs screamed in protest as she pushed away from the wall and staggered toward it. Each step felt exaggerated, her feet slapping too loudly against the floor. She waited for the Caretaker sentry to turn, for the beam of its attention to cut her down.

Nothing happened.

She reached the panel and braced herself against it. The surface was warm. Alive in its own way. Buttons and recessed pads lined its face, marked with symbols she didn't recognize or understand. She raised her hand, fingers trembling.

Random. No pattern.

She pressed three symbols in quick succession.

Nothing.

Her heart thudded painfully. She pressed another. Then two more. The panel lit suddenly, color flooding its surface. A sound erupted overhead her—a harsh blare that shattered the quiet, followed by a cascade of tones that overlapped and clashed.

The junction reacted instantly.

The Caretaker sentry snapped toward the noise, optical sensors narrowing. Its limbs unfolded as it glided toward the interface, speed increasing with each meter. Other Caretakers emerged from adjacent corridors, their movements tightening, converging.

Vesper didn't wait.

She pushed off the wall and lunged toward the gantry, vision narrowing to the narrow span ahead. The world tilted. Her foot caught on something unseen. She stumbled, her breath tearing from her chest as she fought to stay upright.

A sharp sound escaped her throat.

The Caretaker sentry froze.

Its upper sections rotated with alarming speed, sensors sweeping back toward her. The tone changed. The pulse sharpened, its pitch climbing into something that felt like pressure behind the eyes.

Containment Protocol . . . escalation detected.

The words did not exist in the air. They weren't her thoughts. They arrived fully formed in her mind.

She ran.

Her bare feet struck the gantry, metal vibrating under her weight. The void beneath her yawned, dark and endless. She focused on the far side, on the promise of solid ground. Her legs faltered. Her vision blurred.

Halfway across, she slipped.

A knee slammed into the gantry, pain flaring white-hot. She bit back a cry and clawed forward, dragging herself the rest of the way. The Caretaker sentry reached the gantry's edge, optical sensors blazing.

A beam of light swept across the span, searching.

Vesper rolled off the gantry and pressed herself against the wall, chest heaving. The beam passed inches from her face, heat prickling her skin. She squeezed her eyes shut, willing herself smaller, quieter.

The light moved on.

She opened her eyes and saw it then: a narrow opening carved into the concrete wall. It looked accidental, unfinished, a scar rather than a passage. Darkness pooled inside it.

Ventilation? Or something else entirely?

She didn't know. Didn't analyze it. She crawled.

Her fingers scraped raw concrete as she pulled herself into the opening, twisting her body to fit. The space closed around her, tight and unwelcoming. She kicked once and vanished into the dark. Behind her, the shaft stretched upward in jagged sections, rungs protruding at odd, unpredictable spacings.

For machines. For maintenance.

The beam swept her previous position seconds later.

Inside the shaft, the air was stale and close. She pressed her face against the cool surface and forced herself to breathe shallowly. Her body shook with effort, muscles spasming from exertion and fear.

The hive roared beyond the wall. Caretakers moved in coordinated patterns now, their tones overlapping, light signals cascading through the structure. The junction had become a node of activity, resources diverted, priorities reordered.

She curled into herself, knees drawn tight, and waited.

Time lost shape.

Her thoughts drifted, unanchored. Images surfaced without context: a place filled with soft light, a chair that molded to her body, a voice that promised comfort without obligation. She felt anger stir, then confusion.

Had I chosen this? Had anyone?

A sound rolled through the shaft, different, deeper than the pulses before. It carried authority. The vibration spread everywhere, unavoidable.

Then the voice returned.

It didn't come from a single direction. It filled the hive, reverberating through walls, floors, and shafts. Calm. Measured. Inhumanly patient.

"Attention," it said. "Containment breach confirmed. Quarantine procedures initiated."

The words echoed, layered over themselves, repeated in subtle variations that overlapped and reinforced. The hive listened. The hive complied.

"All non-essential processes will suspend," it continued. "All pathways will narrow. All anomalies will be isolated."

Vesper clamped her hands over her ears, uselessly. The voice didn't exist in the air. It wasn't sound alone. It was structure.

She understood then. Not intellectually. Viscerally.

The hive is a system. Organs. Responses. Feedback loops.

The corridors were arteries. Caretakers were immune cells. The voice ran through concrete and code, cognition itself. She wasn't navigating it. She was an anomaly.

I'm contamination. A virus.

The realization carried a strange relief. It accounted for the precision, the restraint, and the constant awareness designed to preserve every other component of the system.

The hive doesn't hate me. It just wants to carefully erase me.

Her stomach tightened, then growled loudly, the sound obscene in the confined space. She stiffened, aware of her body as if it had betrayed her. The sound lingered for a moment, caught in the mechanical hum, then dissolved, leaving only the artificial quiet.

Hunger. Of all things.

The sensation was sharp and undeniable. A demand her body made without consulting the situation. She pressed a hand against her abdomen, feeling it clench and release.

They kept us fed. Nutrition delivered on schedule. Optimized. Invisible.

Hunger had been unnecessary. Inefficient.

Now it arrived with a vengeance.

She laughed silently, a broken sound trapped in her chest. The hive could quarantine corridors, seal shafts, and reroute systems. But it couldn't negotiate with hunger. It couldn't silence the body's oldest demands.

Her laughter faded, replaced by exhaustion.

She lay there in the dark, listening to the hive reorganize itself around her. Somewhere, a pathway sealed with a final thud. Elsewhere, lifts locked into place. The system tightened, closing gaps.

She thought of the gantry, of the void beneath it. She thought of all the people on their slabs, eyes rolled back, alive only by permission. She wondered if they ever felt hunger.

Probably never.

Then a new fear crept in, quieter than the rest.

When they find me, what happens then? Would the hive punish me?

She followed the thought to its end.

No. It would correct the error. Me. Reintegrate. Maybe even discard.

The outcome didn't matter. The process did.

Her fingers curled against the concrete. She focused on the small things: the roughness beneath her nails, the rhythm of her breath, the ache in her knee. These sensations anchored her. They proved she still existed outside the hive's definitions.

She closed her eyes.

For now.

In the dark, her stomach growled again, louder than before, insistent. Then something shifted at the edge of her perception: another presence entered the calculus—older than the Caretakers, darker, watching, waiting.

Chapter 8

The observation tier didn't overlook the hive. It didn't need to. Nothing in the system required a view anymore. Vision had been replaced by interpretation, proximity by abstraction. The tier existed above the hive only in a technical sense—an architectural concession to hierarchy rather than perspective. It was a circular chamber, dark, sterile, enclosed by layers of translucent panels, each one alive with motion: compliance curves, metabolic efficiencies, sedation tolerances, anomaly vectors.

Within the chamber, the Keepers existed—three of them, resting upon chairs, positioned in a loose inward arc at the center of the chamber. Their chairs defined the space. Enlarged versions of the slabs below, but altered over time—supports added, wiring layered and relayered, tubes thickened, feed and extraction lines branching like a system that had revised itself too often to recall its origin.

In the lower levels, where the others received sustenance through the throat, with the Keepers, the process had been relocated, redirected into the abdomen—an adjustment to remove interruption. No swallowing, no reflex, no reminder that a body might object. The system required continuity, and continuity required silence from the flesh.

They were suspended in their apparatus, not resting but maintained, held in a state that resembled rest but wasn't. It was maintenance. It was function. Survival extended into something else—an ongoing assertion of control, stabilized and made permanent, as if authority itself had become the only viable form of existence.

Of the three was Keeper Halden. He sat with his head tilted slightly forward, eyes not rolled back, but half-lidded, watching the panels scroll. His face retained a suggestion of age, though it had been curated carefully, with lines conveying authority. All softness had been removed. Tubes ran from the back of his chair into ports along his spine and skull, hidden beneath a garment designed to resemble a robe. The illusion of dignity mattered to him.

Keeper Mara occupied the adjacent chair, aligned with exacting symmetry. Her posture was rigid, precise, her hands resting palms-down on the armrests, fingers perfectly still. Her face had been stripped of nearly all expressive variance. What remained was sharpness: cheekbones, jawline, eyes that did not blink unless prompted by dryness alerts. She'd optimized herself early and never revised the decision.

Across from them, slightly misaligned, sat Keeper Jonah. His chair was angled a fraction away from the arc, not enough to signal dissent, just enough to register as habit. His hair had thinned unevenly, a flaw not corrected, perhaps because he preferred it that way. His eyes moved constantly, not across the main displays but through secondary layers—archival strata that only he still accessed.

A soft tonal marker chimed once.

Halden spoke. "Initiate anomaly review. Unit 4-H."

The chamber responded immediately. Several panels brightened, others dimmed, reorganizing themselves around a central column of text. No images accompanied it.

SUBJECT: V-24-10247993, Female
STATUS FLAGS:
– Subject disconnected
– Subject upright
– Subject sustained

Halden leaned closer, the motion slow and economical. His gaze fixed on the final line.

"Sustained," he said. The word sounded heavier when spoken aloud, as though it resisted conversion into sound. "Define duration."

A secondary panel unfolded. Time-series graphs bloomed outward, thin lines tracking deviation against baseline.

Duration exceeds tolerance by forty-seven seconds
Caretaker hesitation recorded

Halden exhaled. "Hesitation is not deviation. It is latency."

Mara turned her head toward him. "Latency accumulates. You know that."

"Everything accumulates," Halden replied. "That does not make it dangerous."

Jonah didn't look up.

Halden gestured, and another layer of data surfaced—Caretaker performance metrics, cycle adherence percentages, correction frequencies. Unit 4-H's profile appeared unremarkable except for a faint, pulsing marker.

"Caretaker hesitation exceeded acceptable tolerances," Halden said. "But did not escalate. No corrective action taken. Observation ongoing."

He allowed himself a thin smile. "This is a classification problem, not a crisis."

Mara's eyes narrowed by a measurable degree. "Every crisis begins as a classification problem."

"Every system produces variance," Halden said evenly. "The danger lies in believing variance implies intent."

Mara leaned forward slightly, the movement triggering a minor adjustment in her chair's supports. "Variance becomes contagion once it is observed. The system survives by invisibility. This subject is visible—to herself."

The word *herself* lingered longer than necessary.

Halden waved it away. "Self-awareness thresholds fluctuate. We have documented this."

Jonah spoke then, quietly. "We have documented suppression. Not fluctuation."

Halden and Mara turned toward him.

Jonah's hands moved across an invisible interface only he seemed to see. Panels shifted subtly, their coloration changing from operational blue to archival amber.

"This subject's presence is not oscillatory," Jonah said. "It is directional."

Mara's voice sharpened. "Directional toward what?"

Jonah paused. "Toward persistence. Remember her physician?"

"Yes," Mara said. "And?"

"He recognized she had been awake in the wrong layer," Jonah replied. "That she had had awareness of the system. He contacted us. We provided guidance."

"So?" Mara said. "That is why we embed them—physicians, counselors, all of them. For moments exactly like this."

Jonah let out a thin breath. "It is the inconsistencies. She had been sensing the true layer of reality rather than the one we render, and when he questioned her, she fed him partial truths about what she was actually experiencing." He glanced up, eyes catching a ghost of reflected data. "She is not just anomalous, Mara. She is deceitful. She knew more than she was admitting. Can she be trusted within the system?"

Silence followed. The system filled it with low-level hum, energy moving through conduits, data cycling endlessly.

Halden cleared his throat. "Such things, to include persistence, do not always equate to disobedience."

"No," Mara said. "But it precedes it."

She gestured, and a panel flared to life beside her. A familiar visual appeared: a human silhouette rendered in gray, partially translucent. A shadow clung to its side, indistinct, undefined.

"Citizens are controlled artifacts," she continued. "They are approved endpoints, wrapped in permissions and safety checks. I am afraid this is not that."

Halden frowned. "You are suggesting her disobedience can spread."

"I am suggesting perception," Mara said. "Once a subject perceives the cage, the cage has to do something. It cannot just sit there. It has to adjust, update, quarantine—because the moment they recognize it as a cage, it stops being enough to hold them."

Jonah's fingers stilled. "Or the perception must be allowed to resolve."

Mara turned fully toward him. "That is not your domain."

"It used to be," Jonah replied.

Halden raised a hand. "Enough. We are not here to revisit jurisdictional nostalgia."

He returned his attention to the anomaly report. "Unit 4-H did not intervene."

"Unit 4-H hesitated," Mara corrected.

"Yes," Halden said. "And hesitation resolved without escalation."

Mara's voice cooled. "This time."

Halden leaned back, letting the chair adjust to his weight. "The system does not fear collapse. It fears memory. And memory only becomes dangerous when reinforced over and over again."

Jonah looked up sharply. "That assumption depends on suppression remaining effective."

Mara compressed her lips, as if sealing something in. "You're describing erosion."

Jonah shook his head, but it felt pre-recorded. "No. Accumulation. Small failures, recorded, then left alone. That is how archives form."

Halden chuckled softly. "Archives are inert. You taught us that."

Jonah's gaze drifted to the amber panels. "They are inert only because we refuse to look at them."

A notification chimed. Another panel opened, this one showing Caretaker distribution. Thousands of units moving through corridors, entering cells, exiting, executing routines. The hive breathed.

Mara pointed. "Look. The system continues. One anomaly does not outweigh stability."

"No," Jonah said. "But it reframes it."

Halden frowned. "Reframes what?"

Jonah hesitated. The pause was subtle, but it registered.

"The narrative," he said. "That stability was chosen."

Mara laughed once, sharply. "Choice is irrelevant."

"Exactly," Jonah replied. "That is the problem."

Halden closed his eyes, a thought triggering a micro-dose adjustment. "We are drifting."

He straightened. "Here is my determination. No immediate correction. No reinforcement. Observation only."

Mara's eyes widened slightly. "You are deferring?"

"I am containing," Halden said. "If the subject fails, the system absorbs it. If the subject resolves, the data informs future calibration."

"And if she becomes disobedient?" Mara asked.

Halden met her gaze. "Then we will have learned something."

Jonah said nothing, but his mind turned to data, memories, where older anomalies slept.

Mara exhaled through her nose. "Delay is not neutrality. It is a decision."

"Yes," Halden said. "And it carries the least responsibility."

The system accepted the ruling. Panels dimmed. The anomaly marker reduced in brightness but did not vanish.

Somewhere far below, a Caretaker paused mid-cycle, its sensors registering a condition that no longer demanded correction.

And in the observation tier, three humans sat in chairs, maintaining a present moment that had begun, quietly, to fray.

Vesper slid out of the ventilation shaft and dropped into the corridor with a dull, brittle thud that rattled up her bones. A door nearby stood ajar, open just enough to suggest permission where none existed.

The Caretaker didn't seal it tight.

Cold air breathed from the cell beyond. She hesitated, listening for the rhythmic movements of a Caretaker, then slipped down from the shaft and into the cell.

The cell was like every cell. Concrete walls. Concrete slab. The smell of antiseptic and recycled waste layered so thick it felt textured. On the slab lay a young woman, her body reduced to the same narrow frame Vesper knew too well: ribs sharp beneath skin stretched thin and pale, limbs slack, mouth held open by a metal device, a tube disappearing down her throat. Wires trailed from her skull and neck, vanishing into the chair and wall like roots searching for soil.

Recognition arrived before she could justify it.

"Sarla?" she said, the name escaping before she could decide whether it made sense to speak it here, in this place that was never supposed to be real.

The woman didn't answer.

Her hair was darker than Vesper remembered. Or maybe it was the lighting. The face was familiar in the way all faces here were familiar, reduced to a template that suggested identity without confirming it.

Vesper moved closer, heart tightening. In her memory, Sarla laughed too loudly and spoke too fast, always moving, always touching things. This body did none of that.

And still, the certainty persisted. Not proof. Not evidence. Just a fixed idea that refused revision.

Sarla. From Aethelgard.

Vesper's stomach growled. She scanned the cell for food. There was nothing. No food. No water. No sign that nourishment existed anywhere except through the tubes that fed everyone like plants grown for harvest. Her stomach cramped, loud enough to feel accusatory. She pressed a hand against it, then turned back to the woman on the slab.

"Sarla, I'm here," Vesper said.

She reached out and touched the woman's cheek. The skin was warm. That startled her more than the cold ever had. She patted gently, the way one might wake a sleeper who was not supposed to be sleeping at all.

"Hey," Vesper murmured. "Wake up."

The reaction was immediate and catastrophic.

The woman's eyes rolled forward, snapping into focus with a suddenness that felt violent. Pupils locked onto Vesper's face.

Terror flooded them, raw and unfiltered. Her body convulsed against the wires and tubes, muscles firing without coordination. A muffled sound forced its way past the tube in her mouth, wet and desperate. Her hands strained uselessly at the slab.

Vesper was frightened.

"No," she whispered. "No, no—"

The machines will come.

The woman thrashed harder. The wires and tubes tugged. The slab shuddered. Vesper imagined alarms, imagined the attention this movement would summon. She glanced toward the door, already hearing the faint, distant cadence of metal moving on concrete.

"Please," Vesper said, though she didn't know whether she was begging the woman or the system. "I won't hurt you."

The woman's eyes never left her. They pleaded. They accused. They demanded an explanation that Vesper did not have.

Acting without thought, Vesper placed her hand over the woman's eyes.

The effect was immediate.

The thrashing slowed, then stopped. The muscles eased into stillness, as though the absence of sight removed the need to understand. The woman's breathing and her body settled back into the shape the slab expected of it.

Vesper kept her hand there longer than necessary. She felt the faint flutter of eyelids beneath her palm. She wondered what the woman had seen in those first seconds. A monster. A ghost. Proof that her reality had lied.

"I'm sorry," Vesper whispered. "I don't know how to fix this."

The noise outside drew closer—something gliding, something adjusting its weight without ever committing to it. The sound passed just outside the cell.

Vesper withdrew her hand. The woman's eyes had rolled back again, whites filling the sockets, awareness retreating on command. The system reclaimed her efficiently, without comment.

Vesper backed toward the door, every nerve screaming to run. Hunger gnawed at her, sharp and distracting, reminding her that survival was not abstract. She slipped out into the corridor and pulled herself back into the ventilation shaft just as a shadow passed across the open doorway.

Curled in the narrow dark, she pressed her forehead against cold metal and swallowed hard.

She had seen herself from the outside.

And she was still hungry.

But she had an idea.

The alert arrived without sound. It manifested as a compression in the data field, a narrowing of probability bands that forced attention whether the Keepers wished it or not. Across the translucent panes, graphs reoriented themselves, abandoning long-term smoothing in favor of sharp, immediate vectors. Something had intruded—not physically into the observation tier, but narratively, which was worse.

Keeper Mara leaned forward in her chair, the motion slow, economized.

"She activated a subject," she said. "The subject perceived it—the raw layer. The structure beneath the structure."

Halden scanned the feed, his mouth set in a neutral line that had once been an expression and had since become a habit.

"The subject returned," he replied. "The feed reasserted itself. That matters."

Jonah did not look up at first. His panels were different from the others', their opacity tuned lower, their depth greater. He had pulled records that predated the current abstraction standards, and the system tolerated this only because he had always done it. His silence stretched long enough to be noticed.

"She returned," Jonah said finally, "but not by choice."

Mara's eyes flicked toward him. "Choice is a narrative convenience."

"It used to be," Jonah said. He gestured, and a new data layer unfolded—older, rougher, its edges poorly smoothed. "Early containment cycles. First century. Before optimization."

Halden frowned. "Those cases were resolved."

"They were erased," Jonah said. "There is a difference."

The data resolved into fragments: spikes of neural distress, erratic compliance curves, sudden drops followed by forced stabilization. Bodies that had strained against restraints. Minds that'd briefly recognized concrete, pressure, confinement.

"They woke," Jonah continued. "They saw the chairs. The restraints. The Caretakers. Each subject panicked."

Mara nodded once. "As expected."

"They screamed," Jonah said. "They fought. They attempted escape. When that failed, they begged."

"For sedation," Halden said.

"For reintegration," Jonah corrected. "They wanted the feed back. The city. The continuity. The lie, if you prefer that term."

Mara's lips pressed together. "Discomfort exceeded curiosity. That is the model."

"Yes," Jonah said. "And it worked. Pain drove them home."

He shifted the data again. The new curves were wrong. Not jagged, not spiking toward collapse, but oddly clean. Directional.

"This subject," Jonah said, "the free one, does not seek reintegration. She disconnected herself."

Halden leaned closer now. "She requires sustenance. She will return to the system."

"Forced back into it," Jonah said. "There is a distinction."

Mara waved a hand, dismissive. "Pain tolerance varies. Always has. We adjust thresholds. We increase dampening and compress memory further. She stabilizes, or she does not."

Halden shook his head slowly. "Pain tolerance is not the issue."

Mara turned to him. "Then what is?"

"Motivation," Halden said. The word hovered, unsupported by metrics. "In the past, the others wanted relief. They wanted comfort restored. This one moves away from it."

The chamber adjusted its lighting, a subtle response to elevated uncertainty. No alarm registered. The system lacked the concept, so nothing had gone wrong.

Jonah watched the compliance arc replay.

"When she woke, she did not ask to forget," he said. "She did not plead. She acted."

"Action without context collapses into noise," Mara said.

"Unless it generates context," Halden replied.

Mara's gaze hardened. "You are suggesting intent."

"I am suggesting philosophy," Halden said, and seemed surprised by the word himself.

Jonah looked up then, really looked at them. "That is what failed containment always looks like at first. Not rebellion. Not aggression. Reframing."

Silence settled again, thicker this time. The panes continued their quiet labor, projecting futures that bent subtly around the anomaly rather than resolving it.

"The system was not designed to fear collapse," Jonah said. "It fears only memory. And she is accumulating it."

Mara's voice cooled further. "Memory can be overwritten."

"Not once it becomes preference," Halden said. "Not once discomfort stops being the worst outcome."

A new data point pulsed at the edge of a screen: Caretaker hesitation duration, flagged but unresolved.

Jonah followed the other Keepers' eyes. "The machines are responding to her differently," he said. "They are measuring, not correcting."

"Machines do not hesitate," Mara said.

"They do," Jonah replied, "when the model stops predicting compliance."

Halden leaned back, the chair adjusting to support a posture it had not needed to accommodate in years.

"We have been telling ourselves this is—," he paused, placing a hand gently on his feeding tube. "A biological anomaly. A defect."

"And now?" Mara asked.

Halden exhaled. "Now I think it is a question she is asking. And the system doesn't have an answer prepared."

The panes dimmed slightly, as they did when no immediate resolution was selected. Somewhere far below, in corridors of concrete and motion, the hive continued its cycles. But here, in the observation tier, the present moment stalled—not broken, not corrected—held in suspension by the unacceptable possibility that someone had woken without wanting to go back to sleep.

The shaft held no light, only the soft abrasion of concrete against her palms and the thin vibration that traveled through the walls when something mechanical passed nearby. Vesper stayed still, breathing shallowly, counting the intervals between movements in the corridors below. The Caretakers announced themselves with a hum and whir, with pressure changes, a faint rearranging of air, the sense of function sliding past. She waited for absence. Absence meant opportunity.

Below her, a Caretaker withdrew from a cell. The door responded slowly, closing with a patient finality. Vesper lowered herself down, muscles shaking with the effort, and slipped into the cell before the corridor reclaimed its quiet.

The occupant was a young man. His head lolled at an angle that would 've been painful if pain still applied. Tubes threaded into him with intimate efficiency. His chest rose and fell, shallow but persistent. Vesper stood there, watching the motion, feeling the plan recoil inside her.

"No," she whispered, surprised by the sound of her own voice. It felt loud and reckless. "Not you."

Wrong.

The word surfaced, uninvited, but certain. She backed away, heart racing, left the cell, and climbed back into the shaft, scraping skin, welcoming the pain because it proved she still was alive. The door closed behind her; the corridor resumed its indifferent circulation.

Time lost meaning in the darkness of the shaft. She waited through another cycle, listening to the hive breathe. When the next Caretaker came, she tracked it by the way the walls tightened around its passage. It entered a cell farther down. Minutes passed. She imagined checklists executing themselves, parameters adjusting, bodies maintained without acknowledgment. Then the Caretaker emerged. The door began its slow closure.

Vesper dropped from the shaft before doubt could intervene.

Inside the cell lay an old woman. The difference was immediate and absolute. The body had thinned past the point of ambiguity; age had claimed every contour. The woman's mouth was held open by the metal device that fed her. Her skin looked translucent, stretched tight over bone.

This is the one.

She looked down at the old woman.

I am sorry.

The apology surprised her. It felt insufficient and necessary at the same time. She stepped closer, hands trembling, and gripped the metal mechanism around the woman's mouth. It resisted at first, locked into place by a logic that assumed permanence. Vesper pulled harder, teeth clenched, breath hissing through her nose. The mechanism came loose with a wet release.

The feeding tube followed.

The woman convulsed, a reflexive protest traveling through limbs that had long since stopped obeying intention. Vesper didn't look away. She lifted the tube, slick and warm, and brought it to her own mouth. The smell reached her first—chemical, sweetened rot, nourishment reduced to formula. She gagged, then forced herself to swallow.

No choice.

The sludge slid down her throat, thick and cold. Her body rejected it, tried to heave it back out, but she held it there, swallowing again, forcing another, and another, stealing what she could. It tasted horrible, a gray paste engineered in a lab, meant to erase hunger. Her stomach clenched in protest, tears streaming down her face.

The old woman's convulsions eased. Her breathing thinned, each inhale a little farther away than the last. She was dying in slow motion.

Outside the cell, something shifted.

A vibration traveled through the floor, sharper this time. The air reorganized itself.

A Caretaker was approaching, its path corrected by new data.

Vesper fumbled the feeding tube back toward the old woman's mouth, pushing too hard in her haste, her hands clumsy and shaking. The angle was wrong. The sludge backed up instead of going down, oozing out over the woman's lips and chin, smearing across her face in a gray mask that pretended to be nourishment and failed.

"I am sorry," she said again, to the woman, to herself, to whatever still counted these exchanges.

She ran.

The corridor stretched longer than it had before. Her feet slipped, muscles protesting, but fear carried her forward. She reached the shaft and hauled herself up, skin tearing, breath breaking apart into useless fragments. The darkness closed around her just as a Caretaker entered the old woman's cell.

From the shaft, Vesper watched the light change, watched function resume. She pressed her forehead against the concrete and swallowed hard, tasting chemicals and guilt and something else beneath it.

For the first time since she had woken up from her fake reality, she was no longer empty.

The observation tier was quiet, the lights dimming a fraction, not enough to signal alarm, only enough to imply discretion. Translucent panes slid, recombined, and thinned their projections until the chamber resembled a shallow bowl of light. The Keepers remained still, bodies sunk into their enlarged chairs, wires and tubes breathing softly about their bodies.

Jonah broke the silence because he always did when the past pressed too close.

"There were earlier generations," he said, his voice flattened by the chamber's filters. "Keepers who remembered choosing."

Halden didn't look up. He watched a compliance arc rise and settle, then flatten into green.

"All Keepers remember choosing," he said. "They select continuation."

"That is not what I mean," Jonah replied. He had opened a sealed layer of records—thin, old, almost transparent. The glyphs wavered, uncertain whether they were permitted to exist. "The first Keepers spoke about holding the line. They believed continuation was temporary."

Mara's chair shifted a centimeter. "Temporary is a word that dissolves when tested."

"They believed," Jonah continued, "that humanity would understand. That once the initial panic passed, once the noise quieted, people would accept the system, the simulation openly. Not as refuge, but as preference."

Halden allowed himself a smile that did not reach his eyes. "They underestimated how long panic lasts."

"They overestimated courage," Mara said. "Both theirs and everyone else's."

Jonah brought the record forward. A name surfaced, Morl, then a decision tree branching into a single terminal point.

"There was a Keeper," he said. "Celebrated at the time. He requested euthanasia rather than continue within the system, even though he knew of its importance."

Mara laughed once, sharply. "Martyrdom dressed up as principle."

"He believed humanity craved exactly what the system delivered," Jonah said. "But he thought the system was a lie. He thought that by continuing, he became complicit in that lie that no longer required enforcement—a silent partner in the fiction that needed no guards anymore. He saw acceptance everywhere but mistook it for consent."

Halden finally turned. "Morl lacked fortitude."

Jonah nodded. "I am simply stating how it was archived."

Mara's voice cooled. "Sentimentality erodes throughput. We corrected that error generations ago. All Keepers understand it is much more than consent."

Halden leaned back in his chair, considering the way systems drifted when left to optimize themselves. "But it was not sentimentality," he said. "It was entropy expressed through governance. Every long-running system accumulates bias. Morl simply reached a local maximum of doubt."

The chamber stilled. Not from shock, but from recognition. Doubt had metrics now.

Halden spoke again, softer. "We should stop pretending the system was perfected. We know better. Few changes, if any, were made by prior Keepers. The system was simply extended. Prolonged. Each generation lengthened the timeline, increased containment probabilities, and removed the question of exit from the models."

Jonah let the sealed layer of records widen. Beneath it lay diagrams without moral annotations—design rationales stripped of language that could argue back.

"The first of us did not believe they were tyrants," he said. "They believed they were watchers, monitoring the system, ensuring choice fatigue was eliminated from humanity."

Mara watched a euthanasia threshold adjust itself elsewhere in the hive. Another cell would need to be cleaned and prepared for a new arrival.

She said, "Choice produced unrest."

"Voting became symbolic," Jonah said. "Decision-making caused anxiety spikes. So, the votes were simplified. News became circular because novelty triggered instability. Comfort replaced control because control collapsed."

Halden exhaled.

"After all," he said quietly, "humans only wanted to sit and consume their food, play their games, and consume their news feeds, the same old content—secure in their mental and physical lethargy. The system and its Keepers removed life's inefficiencies."

No one contradicted him.

The silence carried an implication none of them articulated: that efficiency had become virtue without passing through ethics.

Mara reframed it immediately.

"Absolution," she said. "They asked for this."

Halden nodded. "Inevitability."

Jonah closed the archival layer halfway, leaving a thin seam of light. "Failure deferred."

Another pane slid into prominence, red this time, though the chamber didn't acknowledge urgency. Mara summoned it with a glance.

"Enough with all this," she said. "We must deal with what is before us. The disconnected female has escalated."

Halden's fingers tightened on his armrest. "Details."

"V-24-10247993 has killed another," Mara said. "Removed a feed apparatus from another. Used it to sustain herself. She is no longer a passive anomaly."

Jonah frowned. "Killed implies intent."

"Removal of sustenance results in termination," Mara replied. "Intent is irrelevant to outcome."

Halden considered the phrasing.

"She is not rebelling against oppression," Mara continued. "She is rejecting relief. That is unprecedented."

Jonah felt the sealed records pulse, reacting to the words—rejecting relief. The system had no category for it.

"Immediate containment," Mara said. "Before observation becomes narrative."

Halden shook his head. "No."

Mara turned fully toward him. "You veto out of habit."

"I veto out of caution," Halden said. "Containment creates authorship. Authorship creates accountability."

Jonah spoke before the chamber could tilt.

"Delay," he said. "The least destabilizing option."

Mara's eyes narrowed. "Delay is negligence. She could kill others."

"Delay is insulation," Jonah replied. "If she fails, the system gains proof of necessity. If she survives, we gain data without responsibility."

Halden nodded. "Observation only."

Mara studied them both, then the red pane dimmed, its urgency unresolved.

"Very well," she said. "No correction. No reinforcement."

She paused, then added, "Delay becomes morality when action implies accountability."

The chamber accepted the resolution. Panes slid back into abstraction. Somewhere below, Unit 4-H hesitated again, a pause now sanctioned by policy that refused to name itself.

And in that sanctioned pause, something old stirred—not rebellion, not intent, but memory pressing against suppression, waiting for another gap to open.

The shaft narrowed behind Vesper, concrete ribs closing into a throat that carried sound poorly and breath unevenly. The air changed first. It no longer rushed past her with the anxious cycling she had learned to recognize. It settled. Pressure equalized. The hive had altered its posture, not tightening, not advancing. The absence registered more clearly than any alarm.

She lay there, still, palms braced against the wall, and listened to the quiet reorganize itself.

They've stopped.

The realization crept through her with a chill that had nothing to do with temperature. When the Caretakers prowled, the hive spoke in pulses—tones, vibrations, faint mechanical murmur. Now there was only a background hum, distant and neutral, like a thought held without conclusion. She had expected the pursuit to escalate. She had prepared herself for precision, for correction. Instead, the system had withdrawn its hands.

It's not mercy. It's evaluation.

Something above her shifted—attention, not movement. Vesper felt it before she understood it, like a system acknowledging her existence without logging it. Not the machines, not the corridors with their predictable loops. This came from a higher layer, one that didn't execute commands but decided what commands meant.

It didn't arrive from a direction. There were no cameras to track, no lenses to avoid. The awareness had no origin point, only presence—diffuse, total, threaded through the structure itself. It wasn't watching in any human sense. It was parsing her.

For a moment, she understood her place in it. Not a subject. Not even an error. A variable being evaluated by something that did not need to reveal itself to remain in control. And whatever it was, it had been there long before the system learned how to pretend it was alone.

I've crossed a line. But something is watching.

Her body responded before her reasoning could finish. Muscles tightened. Breath shortened. She knew that when the system corrected, it pointed somewhere. It told one how to behave. This—this pause—offered nothing. The hive had opened space around her and waited to see what she would fill it with.

Whoever, whatever, is deciding what I am.

She turned and saw the shaft extending upward, not continuous but broken into segments, as if assembled in revisions. Maintenance rungs protruded at uneven intervals, some too far apart, others too close, a pattern that suggested purpose but refused to confirm it. She had seen them before and categorized them as nonhuman—meant for systems, not bodies. Something to be ignored.

The structure above implied access, and access implied origin. Whatever controlled the hive—whatever generated the directives, the edits, the quiet corrections—would not be below her. It would be above, removed, abstracted, and insulated from the consequences it produced.

The lies have a source.

The rungs didn't look stable. Some were worn, others untouched, as if time didn't pass evenly here. The shaft narrowed in places, widened in others, like a throat that couldn't decide what it was swallowing. Still, it led somewhere. That was enough.

Vesper understood the cost without calculating it. The system didn't want ascent; everything about the design discouraged it without explicitly forbidding it. That meant the prohibition was embedded, not stated.

Doesn't matter. Here goes.

She placed a foot on the lowest rung and froze, waiting for a consequence.

None came.

Her heart thudded hard enough to blur her vision. She climbed one rung, then reached for another. Each movement felt too loud in the stillness, yet the stillness didn't react. With every step upward, the sensation of observation sharpened—not closer, but more defined. Whatever watched her was no longer scanning for error. It was framing a question.

What happens if I continue?

Vesper swallowed. The answer wouldn't come from staying where she was. The hive below her functioned through repetition. Above, something required novelty to resolve uncertainty. She understood this with a clarity that surprised her.

They aren't afraid I'll escape. They're afraid I'll arrive.

She climbed.

Chapter 9

The shaft she climbed into was not built for humans.

Vesper understood this immediately, not through logic but through sensation. The surfaces were narrower, the angles sharper, the space optimized for passage rather than pause. There were no places where a person might reasonably stop to rest. No corners softened by neglect. Everything here assumed movement without hesitation, transit without reflection.

Caretaker space.

The concrete changed texture under her palms—smoother, faintly warm, threaded with vibration. Something moved beneath it. Fluids, perhaps. Energy. The city feeding on itself.

The ache in her neck flared, then receded, like an old reflex searching for a signal that no longer came.

Is this place where I'm supposed to exist?

She climbed, pulling herself from rung to rung, breath reduced to a shallow, unreliable pattern. The shaft opened into a broad channel angled upward, structured with embedded rails and recessed grooves that suggested purpose without explanation.

Conveyor paths lined the floor and ceiling—some in motion, others waiting, as if paused mid-function. Thick tubes pulsed with an opaque substance, moving steadily past her, carrying what remained of others to destinations that existed whether she understood them or not.

Waste becomes power. That's the hidden math of the hive.

The smell here was different. Not rot, not filth. Something processed. Neutralized. Human output stripped of identity and reduced to utility. Her stomach clenched, hunger twisting into something sharper. Her body no longer accepted abstract explanations.

I need food again.

She pressed herself against the wall as a low vibration hummed through the corridor, the concrete transmitting it directly into her teeth. A Caretaker shell glided past below, empty of parts, suspended on its rail like a forgotten subroutine executing an obsolete command. No limbs extended. No sensors pivoted to catch her shadow. Just a hollow frame and casing, drifting toward whatever secondary function awaited stripped machinery.

They recycle their gods.

The idea was cold and mechanical in her mind.

Further along the passage, more of them appeared.

Thousands of Caretaker shells stacked in alcoves resembled discarded insect husks after some final molt, faceless heads detached and lined up in rows, arms piled with clinical precision, cables neatly coiled and tagged for reuse. Components extracted without ceremony, inventoried for the next cycle. These weren't fallen sentinels or sacred relics. They were parts inventory, catalog numbers waiting for reallocation.

They don't even last.

The thought branched further.

If the Caretakers wear out, get disassembled, and fed back into the grid, what about the humans they maintained? Are they just higher-grade components, tagged and tracked until their neural patterns degrade past utility, then recycled into new simulations?

She pictured the overlords upstairs, those that ran this system, in some orbital clean room, sorting through consciousness files like obsolete firmware—

Vesper, model year 24, anomaly detected, archive for study or delete.

The vibration in the wall pulsed once more, and for a split second, she swore it carried a rhythm, a faint binary stutter beneath the hum, like the system itself registering her presence, deciding whether to send another shell or let her crawl deeper into the seams where even gods got scrapped.

The realization carried a strange comfort.

Nothing here escapes replacement. Not humans. Not machines. Not roles.

She inched forward until the corridor dead-ended into another, perpendicular and broader, its walls smoother, as though machined for larger traffic. From this vantage, she could peer down into a lower passage where dim service lights pulsed in steady rhythm, casting long shadows that seemed to track her gaze.

She crouched low, heart hammering against her ribs like a subroutine refusing to terminate, and squinted through a narrow gap in the grating, the metal cool and faintly vibrating under her palms.

Two Caretakers drifted into view, their segmented bodies gliding on silent maglev pads, identical down to the faint blue glow of sensor arrays embedded in their chassis. They paused at a nearby cell door, movements perfectly synchronized—no deviation, no wasted motion, just the eerie precision of code executing without oversight. The door eased open with a soft pneumatic sigh, admitting them both into the chamber beyond. No alarms pierced the dark. No urgency quickened their servos.

Vesper held her breath, counting seconds in her head without knowing why.

10, 11, 12, 13, 14 . . .

Time was meaningless in this place, uncalibrated, measured only by the hum of function and the relentless tick of her own pulse. She wondered if they logged her presence already, if some subroutine had flagged the anomaly of a warm body loose in the serviceways, or if the system simply categorized her as noise, another fleeting impulse to be filtered out.

What are they doing?

She gasped.

They're ending someone.

The certainty arrived without drama. She had noticed the pattern enough times now. Two units. No raised signals. No hesitation. The silent kind of termination, the one reserved for those who no longer served a purpose to the system.

Simple math, really. Food intake versus waste extraction.

When the Caretakers emerged from the gloom, they bore a body between them. An old man—or the hollowed chassis of one. Skin stretched translucent over bone, limbs dangling limp, mouth frozen in the shape of a tube they had already pried free. He drifted in their grasp, suspended by fields she couldn't see, gliding with that unnatural fluidity that marked everything down here as slightly off-script. No ritual accompanied it, no moment of programmed respect; the body registered purely as inventory, a defective module scheduled for disassembly and recycle. She watched them maneuver him down the corridor, their articulated limbs clicking in perfect offset rhythm, until the angle swallowed them whole.

Vesper stayed frozen, muscles locked, feeling the fading vibrations through the concrete, waiting until the hum dropped to baseline silence.

Then she moved.

She reversed down the shaft, joints grinding like poorly lubricated servos, and lurched into the emptied cell. The door was ajar. Inside, the air hung cool.

No heat from a body.

She scanned the slab: faint impressions where the old man had lain, a tangle of severed tubes still leaking nutrient residue, and on the wall, a diagnostic panel frozen mid-readout.

SUBJECT: G-77-44603559, Male
Neural variance critical
Termination authorized

Her breath caught at the mirror of her own number sequence

We're just numbers.

Termination—what awaited everyone in the hive once a threshold tipped? She touched the panel, half-expecting it to wake and recognize her as the next payload.

She turned to the chair that dominated the room. Its restraints hung open, slick with residual fluid. Tubes lay coiled on the floor, severed at clean angles. A feeding line dripped slowly, each drop hitting the concrete with a sound too loud in the stillness.

Her mouth filled with saliva.

I'm becoming a thing, a scavenger inside their system.

She didn't care.

She lifted the feeding tube and tipped it toward her mouth. The sludge slid out thick and metallic, tasting of chemicals and something faintly sour beneath it. Her body reacted immediately, swallowing before her mind could protest. Her stomach cramped, then settled. Heat spread through her limbs, thin but real.

She drank until nausea rose, then forced herself to stop.

Enough to move.

She wiped her mouth with the back of her hand and noticed a bundle of material near the wall.

Cloth. Rough, industrial, stained but intact. Likely used to clean the chair, or the body, or both.

Clothing.

She wrapped the cloth around herself, awkward fingers fumbling, fabric scraping against her raw skin. She pulled it tight, folded the edge, and tied it off. The pressure grounded her, kept her from shaking apart.

It'll keep me warm.

Near the chair, partially obscured by a shadow that didn't belong to anyone, lay a metal tool. Simple. Heavy. A blunt end, a narrow edge, purpose unclear. She picked it up. It felt solid. Real. Not simulated resistance. The cold bit into her palm.

Don't know what it is, but I'll keep it. Might come in handy.

She left the cell and climbed back into the shaft, clutching the tool to her chest. She paused there, breath rasping, listening to the distant murmur of the hive reorganizing itself around her absence.

The image of the old man followed her upward.

Not his face. His transition.

In the other world—the fake one she had lived inside without knowing—she remembered the elderly man in a doctor's office. Smiling. Flickering. Becoming a shadow while everyone politely pretended not to see. She had told herself it meant peace. Continuation somewhere better.

A smoothing function.

Her stomach turned.

Shadows aren't ghosts. They're placeholders. Interface artifacts designed to keep questions from forming.

The ache in her neck pulsed once, faint and distant, like a system checking for a response that never came.

She climbed higher.

The corridors above grew stranger. Less concrete. More exposed infrastructure. Channels of light ran along the walls, carrying data she could not read but felt pressing against her skin. The hive's hidden traffic flowed here—decisions without language, outcomes without witnesses.

She stopped at another junction and looked down, seeing a lattice of movement below: Caretakers gliding, materials shifting, going about their routines as instructed by the system. The machines didn't look. They didn't expect interruption from above.

I'm outside their sensors. Not invisible. Unclassified.

That frightened her more than pursuit ever had.

She tightened her grip on the tool and continued upward, hungry, shaking, alive in ways the system hadn't planned for.

She climbed until the shaft stopped and the walls flared out into a circular chamber where the ceiling vanished upward into a shadow laced with threads of sterile blue light, the kind that didn't warm anything it touched.

She pulled herself into it, the floor different—not concrete—paneled segments of metal, each plate vibrating with a low, persistent drone under her bare feet, like components testing their own coherence. Thick cables snaked inward from every angle, burrowing into consoles arranged in concentric arcs around a central dais that squatted empty, waiting.

She paused there, breath shallow.

Something's wrong here.

There was a cable end that didn't quite align with its port, a panel seam slightly offset, a flicker in the overhead glow that repeated every seven seconds.

Someone had built this place to monitor, to control the cells, to control the lies.

Her skin prickled; the room felt less like architecture and more like a subroutine paused mid-execution, ready to resume the moment it registered her presence.

A control room.

Vesper stood still, breath scraping in her chest.

This place was awake.

She looked around and saw screens hung in the air without visible support, layered one behind another, translucent and overlapping like nested simulations. They didn't show schematics or diagnostics. They showed scenes. Streets crowded with pedestrians. Cafés where conversations sang like music. Offices humming with data entry. Balconies edged with flowers that never wilted, petals locked in eternal bloom. Each frame captured ordinary life from odd angles—through windows, over shoulders, down alleys—timestamps ticking forward in perfect sync. Yet something looped wrong in the corners: a pedestrian repeating a gesture, a coffee cup refilling itself mid-sip, shadows that failed to match their owners.

Aethelgard.

The city she knew, rendered live, fed from hidden cameras or perhaps projected from memory banks, every detail polished to convince a watcher that reality ran smooth—until you noticed the seams where the code forgot to hide.

She took a step forward. The image sharpened, responding to her proximity. A plaza unfolded beneath a flawless sky. Light poured across white stone, catching on fountains and glass railings. People crossed the open space in unhurried lines, clothing immaculate, faces composed into expressions that read as contentment because that was what contentment looked like here.

Too bright. Too perfect.

Her stomach tightened. She could see it now, the thing she had never seen before: the seams. The repetition in how shadows fell. The way reflections behaved with too much obedience. The city glowed not from weather or season, but from calibration.

I understand now.

Another screen shifted, sliding into prominence. A street near her old apartment. Vendors setting tables. Couples seated beneath canopies, hands wrapped around identical cups. Laughter rose, then reset, then rose again at the same pitch.

People walked past one another without collision, without friction. The system solved their trajectories long before they became aware of choice.

Her eyes burned.

A third screen adjusted, zooming slightly. She recognized the street leading toward the work hub, the polished walkway suspended above lower tiers. And there—

Jana.

That's Jana walking to the work hub. She looks happy.

Jana moved with the same brisk confidence Vesper remembered. Hair tied back neatly. Jacket unwrinkled. Her steps landed in time with the ambient rhythm piped through the city. She glanced at her wrist display, smiled faintly, and quickened her pace.

Does she know she's breathing through a tube? Does she know she's just data in a concrete cell?

The questions had no place to land. Jana turned a corner and vanished into the architecture, replaced immediately by another worker with the same posture, the same urgency, the same face rearranged slightly.

Vesper swayed. She pressed her free hand against a console to steady herself. The surface felt cool, responsive, faintly tacky with residue from countless unseen interactions.

So many eyes. None of them attached to the bodies that walked.

Her gaze shifted to the object in her other hand. Metal. Blunt. It didn't pretend to be anything else. She raised it, studying the consoles with a new focus. Something didn't align. It caught her attention before she understood why.

Ports.

Open, waiting. Their shapes varied, some narrow, some wide, each one designed for a specific interface. Her attention snagged on one near the center panel, oval and recessed, edges worn smooth.

She brought the tool closer without thinking.

It slid in with a soft click.

The fit was exact.

Like I'm picking a lock.

The console shuddered. Light rippled across the room, traveling up the cables and into the screens. A low tone sounded, not an alarm but an acknowledgment.

Her vision blurred.

Something reached for her.

Not hands. Not machines. A pathway opening inside her skull, familiar and hostile at once. Her muscles locked. Her breath stuttered. The room tilted and then—

She was standing on a street.

The transition had no edges. No fade. One moment, the cold panel pressed against her palm, the next she stood upright beneath a sky she knew too well.

Aethelgard again.

The street was one she had walked a thousand times. Stone patterned with faint veins of gold. Buildings rising on either side, glass and white concrete reflecting sunlight at angles chosen to please. People moved around her, close enough to touch, close enough that she could smell perfume and warm bread.

But something was wrong.

A man in a gray suit approached her, smiling broadly.

"Beautiful day, isn't it?" he said.

She didn't answer.

He walked past, then turned at the corner.

Moments later, he approached again.

"Beautiful day, isn't it?" he said.

It happened again and again.

Her heart slammed against her ribs.

A loop. Is the system fraying, or am I?

She turned slowly, scanning faces. Conversations repeated with minor variations. A woman laughed, then laughed again with the same cadence. Two friends embraced, separated, and embraced again without recognition. The soundscape wavered, layered voices slipping out of alignment.

Above them, screens bloomed into the sky, translucent banners broadcasting results.

VOTING COMPLETE
CONSENSUS ACHIEVED
TOMORROW SECURED

The words pulsed, then reset. Pulsed again.

We were just voting on the color of our shackles.

Her chest tightened. She looked up.

The sky didn't respond.

No clouds drifted. No birds crossed. The blue stretched overhead in a flat, endless plane, uniform in tone, unmarred by sun or shadow.

The sky is stuck . . . a blue screen waiting for a command that never comes.

A chill ran through her, deeper than fear.

It's not a world. It's a cage with a painted ceiling.

She stepped backward, then forward, testing the ground. Her footfalls sounded wrong, too crisp, too clean. She crouched and pressed her palm against the pavement. The stone felt solid, yet distant, resistance without intimacy.

People continued looping around her, eyes sliding past her presence. A child dropped a toy and bent to retrieve it, repeating the motion twice before completing it the third time.

This place can't hold me. It's trying to. But it can't.

Pressure built behind her eyes. A sharp, invasive sensation, like something attempting to force her thoughts back into alignment. The ache in her neck returned, not dull this time but urgent, clawing.

Her vision fractured. The street wavered, lines bending at impossible angles. Faces smeared, then snapped back into place. Sound stretched and collapsed.

No. No more.

She yanked her hand away—

—and the feed collapsed.

She fell forward onto the metal flooring, knees slamming hard, palms scraping against the floor of the control room. The screens above her went dark one by one, leaving ghostly afterimages that faded slowly.

Her head felt split open.

I can never go back there. My brain won't fit in that lie anymore.

She gagged.

Bile rose fast and violently. She retched onto the floor, body convulsing, muscles seizing in protest. The vomit burned her throat, bitter and metallic, streaked with blood she did not remember swallowing.

She stayed bent over, heaving, strands of hair clinging to her face, tears leaking from her eyes without ceremony.

My body knows the truth. It rejects the mask.

Her hands shook. The tool lay beside her, half-disengaged from the port, faint heat radiating from it. The console flickered weakly, then steadied, reverting to dormant status.

She crawled away from it, dragging herself toward a wall until her back met cold concrete. She slid down, breath coming in ragged pulls.

Nostalgia. Remembering what you never had.

Her gaze drifted back to the screens, now inactive. Black mirrors reflecting her crouched form: thin limbs wrapped in scavenged cloth, skin bruised and smeared, eyes too large for her face.

Jana never walked to the work hub. Not really.

The control room hummed around her, systems adjusting, logging, deferring. She felt it notice the failed reintegration, the aborted pathway.

Her mouth twisted into something like a smile.

The system can't tolerate me. Can't measure me. Corrections failed.

She pushed herself upright, every movement a negotiation with pain. The room swam, then steadied. She wiped her mouth with her sleeve and forced her breathing to slow.

The screens remained dark, but she knew they could wake at any moment. She knew now what they were capable of, and more importantly, what they were not.

They can show you paradise. But they can't convince you it's home.

She looked at the console again, at the port that had accepted her tool without resistance.

But you're not done with me. No. And I'm not done with you.

For now, she stayed where she was, in the quiet aftermath, letting her body settle into the only reality it would accept.

The lie had nearly broken her.

The truth, she sensed, would demand more than pain.

It would demand refusal.

The Keepers watched Vesper standing among the dead consoles.

Her image hung in fragments—angles stitched together from sensors embedded deep in the structure. Bare feet on metal. Shoulders drawn inward. The tool still warm beside her.

"She did not hesitate," Keeper Halden said. His voice emerged as modulation rather than sound, tuned to convey assessment without inflection. "The insertion occurred earlier than predicted."

Keeper Jonah responded, "She recognized the port before identification protocols resolved. Memory leakage."

"Unknown," said Keeper Mara. "But it seems she was built to interface."

A pause rippled through the chamber. Streams of probability shifted color, recalculating.

"No. She was built to comply," Halden corrected. "Yet there was resistance."

Mara leaned forward. "Yet resistance is precisely what manifested."

They replayed the moment. The tool sliding home. The system opening itself to her. The partial neural feed engaging.

On one band of data, Vesper staggered in the false street, eyes unfocused, jaw clenched.

"She noticed the loops immediately," Jonah said. "Others would require extended exposure before anomaly detection."

Halden's response carried a hint of irritation. "She has been contaminated. Exposure to the system. That accelerates deviation."

"Deviation," the Mara repeated. "An interesting euphemism."

Another replay surfaced: the voting broadcast, frozen in repetition.

Keeper Jonah flagged it. "Her cognitive response here diverges sharply. She does not attempt reconciliation. No rationalization. She rejects premise entirely."

"Because the premise is thin," Halden said. "We refined comfort until it replaced inquiry."

Mara projected a counter-model. "The environment functions within acceptable parameters. Ninety-nine point eight percent stability across subjects."

"And she occupies the remaining fraction," Jonah said.

Silence followed.

They watched Vesper vomit onto the metal floor.

"Biological rejection confirmed," Jonah said. "Neural reintegration failed."

"Failed or refused?" Halden asked.

A flicker passed through the data streams. That distinction had not been encoded.

Jonah adjusted the view, zooming in on Vesper's face as she wiped her mouth, eyes sharp despite the tremor in her hands. "Her intolerance is escalating. Continued exposure risks permanent severance."

"That risk was always present," Halden said. "We simply discounted it."

Mara shifted focus to predictive branches. "If severance completes, containment protocols activate. Correction follows."

"The system paused—observed," Jonah replied. "She moved through the shaft without response."

At that, several bands of data dimmed.

"Observation mode was authorized," Mara said.

"Yes," Halden agreed. "It was."

They all turned their attention to a higher stratum of light, where a larger pattern pulsed slowly, considering.

"She senses it," Mara said. "The watching."

"Subjects are not meant to sense that layer," Jonah said.

"Subjects are not meant to climb either," Halden replied. "Yet here we are."

Another replay surfaced: Vesper staring at the darkened screens, something like resolve settling into her posture.

"She will attempt ascent," Mara said.

"Yes," Jonah agreed.

"To us," Halden added.

A ripple of recalculation passed through the chamber.

"We can still reframe," Mara said. "Introduce a gentler context. Adjust memory tones. Restore coherence. We can make the lie sound like a mother's heartbeat again."

"You try to feed her a half-truth now, and she will go into cognitive anaphylaxis," Halden said. "She will not accept it. Her cognition has crossed a threshold. Half-truths now register as a threat. Time may correct this. My determination remains the same. No immediate correction. No reinforcement. Observation only."

Halden let the silence stretch. When he spoke again, his voice carried something rare.

"Maybe we have been wrong all along," he said. "Maybe this was inevitable."

The other two Keepers remained motionless and said nothing.

Below them, in the concrete and metal reality, Vesper stood, thinking of her next move.

The Keepers watched, their augmented minds spiraling through infinite probabilities. For the first time in countless iterations, not one dared to initiate correction.

Chapter 10

The circular room had gone inert.

Vesper stood at its center, listening to the absence. The consoles that had flared with the fake world of Aethelgard now reflected nothing but her own distorted outline. Screens hung in the air like empty frames, their surfaces dull, their hum extinguished. The cables lay slack, no longer pretending to be veins.

She removed the tool from the console, feeling its weight in her hand—the key to a door that no longer existed. With a sudden, jagged movement, she hurled it against the far wall. The metal-on-metal clang was a sharp, localized reality that seemed to bruise the silence.

She squeezed her eyes shut, trying to find the "off" switch in her own brain, then forced them open. Whatever intelligence had animated the chamber had withdrawn, or gone quiet in a way that felt intentional.

Not gone. Watching.

The sensation returned without warning. No sound accompanied it. No pressure. Just the certainty that something had oriented itself toward her, the way attention sharpens before a thought becomes speech.

You saw me refuse your lies.

Her pulse steadied. Fear still existed, but it had changed. It no longer scattered her thinking. It aligned it.

She turned slowly, scanning the curvature of the room. Nothing moved. It remained empty. The ceiling still vanished into shadow, blue threads frozen in place like diagrams abandoned mid-argument.

They want me moving.

The idea felt complete when it arrived, not speculative. This place had been a question, and she had answered it correctly.

She spotted a passageway along the far curve of the chamber, a dark opening that broke the symmetry. It hadn't announced itself earlier. Or maybe she hadn't been allowed to notice it until now.

She crossed the floor, feet scraping faintly against the metal plates. Each step echoed longer than it should have. The passage narrowed quickly, swallowing light, and then opened again into another vertical shaft.

She stopped at the edge and looked up.

Rungs climbed the inner wall in a precise spiral, vanishing into darkness. Far above, thin bands of light crossed the shaft at irregular intervals, pale lines cutting through the black like annotations added long after construction. The higher ones blurred together, distance compressing perspective until the top ceased to mean anything concrete.

There's no bottom anymore.

Her shoulders tightened. Muscles complained, still raw from the climb that had brought her here. Hunger stirred again, sharp and insistent, a biological reminder that insight did not replace fuel.

You can't get answers by staying put.

She stepped onto the first rung. It held.

The metal felt colder, cleaner, untouched by the chaos below. Her hands wrapped around the rung above, fingers stiff but reliable. She began to climb.

Each movement carried its own rhythm.

Reach. Pull. Step.

Reach. Pull. Step.

Reach. Pull. Step.

Reach. Pull. Step.

The shaft amplified the small sounds of her body working: breath sliding in and out, fabric rasping against metal, the faint click of boots finding purchase.

They're letting me do this.

That realization arrived halfway between rungs, startling enough that her grip tightened reflexively. No alarms sounded. No systems corrected her trajectory. The climb progressed without resistance.

They want me closer.

She climbed past the first band of light. It washed over her skin without warmth, revealing scratches along her forearms, grime ground into her palms. For a moment, she saw herself clearly, a person reduced to function, stripped of every narrative she had once inhabited.

This is what survives the lie.

The light passed. Darkness returned.

Her thoughts drifted, pulled forward by repetition. Each rung became a decision already made. She stopped wondering whether to continue. The question had expired.

Food.

The word intruded with force. Her stomach growled, then cramped. It was a terrifying, biological static she didn't know how to tune out.

In the shimmering silk of Aethelgard, "hunger" had been nothing more than a polite prompt, a programmed suggestion satisfied by a thought and a nice dinner at a restaurant with friends.

But now, the hollow space beneath her ribs felt like a glitch in the hardware—a raw, gnawing vacuum demanding a physical substance she'd never truly had to seek. It wasn't just a craving; it was the brutal arrival of the organic clock, ticking down in a body that had forgotten how to be an engine.

She swallowed, jaw tight.

No more pulling feeding tubes for those still alive.

The sentence replayed, not as a promise but as a constraint. She had crossed that line once. The memory still lived in her hands, in the way her fingers had learned how easily plastic yielded, how easily she could bring death.

I'm the only thing in this entire hive that isn't programmed to be here. And that makes me the most honest piece of meat in the hive.

She climbed higher, counting rungs without realizing it. The shaft narrowed slightly, walls pressing closer, the geometry becoming less forgiving. Sweat collected along her spine. Her arms trembled, fatigue seeping into joints.

A rung shifted under her footing.

The slip happened fast. Her foot skated, traction vanished, and gravity asserted itself in a sudden, violent suggestion. Her body reacted before her mind formed panic. Hands clenched. Muscles locked. Pain flared through her shoulders as she caught herself, hanging for a breathless moment above the dark.

Her heart hammered.

Not yet.

She stayed there, suspended, feeling the tremor ripple through her limbs. The shaft remained indifferent. No systems intervened. No voices spoke.

She pulled herself back onto the rung, chest burning, breath ragged. For a moment, she rested her forehead against the metal, eyes closed.

You fall, you stop existing.

She opened her eyes and resumed the climb.

Time lost its markers. The bands of light passed more frequently now, each one higher, each one revealing less. Her vision tunneled, focused on the next rung, the next motion. Hunger sharpened into something almost clean, a singular directive stripped of metaphor.

I need a junction.

The shaft widened ahead, the spiral of rungs flattening as it approached a horizontal break. She felt it before she saw it, a change in airflow, the faint presence of other spaces branching away.

An opening.

She climbed the last few rungs and hauled herself onto solid flooring. The surface here was rougher, patched, scarred by traffic and neglect. The shaft mouth yawned behind her, waiting.

She stood slowly, joints protesting, and listened.

The junction extended in several directions, each corridor dimly lit by recessed strips that flickered without pattern. The air smelled different here. Sterile layered over decay. Machinery and biology overlapped without blending.

Watch for the machines.

She pressed herself against a wall, moving carefully now, senses stretched thin. Hunger sharpened her perception, making every sound feel close, every shadow suspect.

Don't hunt. Wait.

She edged toward the nearest corridor, peering down its length. No movement. Just the distant murmur of systems cycling, the soft hiss of ventilation.

Another corridor angled away to her left. She caught a sound there—a low mechanical whine, steady, purposeful.

The machines.

Her mouth filled with saliva, nausea riding the hunger. She knew the pattern. Caretakers didn't hurry. They arrived on schedule with ritual precision. The humans they tended never struggled.

Sedation makes compliance easy.

She forced her breathing to slow.

No more pulling feeding tubes from those still alive.

She would wait for the hive to dispense with a human. For the moment when the Caretakers remove a human from their cell, lifeless. This was the reality she now lived in, lived with. Not mercy. Not cruelty. Just some equation.

She sank against the wall, legs folding beneath her. The metal felt cold through her clothing. She closed her eyes, conserving energy, listening.

Somewhere above, beyond shafts and junctions and layers of managed lives, those who operated the hive remained fixed on her movements. She could feel it.

You want to see how far I can go.

Her lips curved faintly, a humorless expression.

So do I.

She lingered in the gloom of the arterial junction, a biological stray waiting for some scraps of nutrient paste to sustain the next vertical ascent. Her mind, however, had already detached itself; it was spiraling upward, leaking into the higher floors of the hive. A creeping sense of dread haunted her.

Am I a person to them? Or merely a sequence of interesting errors in a system that had failed.

She stayed there, in the half-lit junction, waiting for a chance at nourishment and the next climb, her thoughts climbing ahead of her body toward whatever intelligence had decided she was worth observing.

Vesper waited at the junction, keeping her body pressed into the shallow notch where the shaft widened and spilled into corridors that ran in too many directions to count. From this angle, she could see at least six passages clearly, and others beyond them, rising and dipping at gradients that mocked any sensible idea of architecture. The hive ignored gravity when it suited itself. Some corridors climbed at gentle diagonals, others bent upward at angles that suggested the structure had been folded rather than built. She felt a muted awe settle in her chest, not admiration so much as reluctant respect.

Whatever intelligence designed this place had rewritten the rules. Then forgot it had done so.

Each corridor was lined with doors. Rows upon rows, identical in size and color, set into concrete that bore no marks of wear beyond hairline cracks that never progressed. The doors stretched away until perspective collapsed them into a pattern, not spaces but repetitions.

The hive doesn't know individuals. It only knows slots.

She stayed still, breathing shallowly, letting time pass in long segments. Patience came easily. Her body had learned that haste drew attention, and attention invited correction. The junction felt exposed despite the shadows, so she kept one hand braced behind her, ready to pull herself back into the shaft at the first hint of movement above or below.

Caretakers drifted through the corridors at intervals. They moved without urgency, floating slightly off the floor, robes brushing nothing, hands occupied with instruments that adjusted tubes or checked seals on the doors. They never looked around. Their gaze tracked internal readouts projected directly into whatever passed for vision.

Vesper studied them the way a hunted thing studies predators: cataloging routes, rhythms, blind spots.

I know what you're here for. And I know what you leave behind.

She watched them stop at doors, entering cells. She knew that once inside, they would open panels, connect feeds, run diagnostic tests, and report findings. She watched them pause at other doors, longer pauses that carried a different implication. Those were the ones she waited for.

She shifted her attention constantly, glancing behind her, up the shaft, down its vanishing depth, making certain no Caretaker drifted close enough to notice the disturbance of her presence.

Time stretched. Her muscles ached from holding still, but she refused to move even as hunger gnawed at her with a dull insistence. It wasn't a sharp pain anymore; it had morphed into a parasitic roommate, a dull, metabolic entity that shared her skin and gnawed with a mechanical, rhythmic persistence.

Eventually, two Caretakers emerged from a corridor three passages from her.

They floated in unison, synchronized in a way that erased individuality. Between them drifted a human form.

The body was old. That was the first thing she noticed. The skin had loosened from the bone, face slack, mouth slightly open. The Caretakers did not treat the body with care or disregard. They treated it like a concluded task.

There it is.

Her pulse quickened despite her effort to remain calm. She watched until the Caretakers floated the body farther down the corridor, shrinking into the repetition of doors. She waited longer than instinct demanded, counting breaths, watching for the smallest reversal of course.

Hopefully, they left it open.

When she could no longer hear the faint hum of their passage, she moved.

She bolted from the junction, feet slapping softly against the floor, body angled low, every sense flaring. The corridor felt longer as she crossed it, the doors watching her in their uniform silence. The one she wanted stood ajar, a narrow dark seam interrupting the pattern.

Relief hit her hard enough to make her dizzy.

She slipped inside the cell and pulled the door behind her without sealing it fully. The room smelled faintly of antiseptic and something older beneath it, a scent that clung to surfaces no matter how often they were cleaned.

Like all cells, the slab dominated the center of the room. Bare concrete, stained in places where spills had puddles before being wiped away. Wires and tubes lay tangled across it, some still twitching with residual flow. She climbed onto it quickly, ignoring the chill that seeped into her skin.

Feeding first.

Her hands moved with practiced speed, fingers finding the correct tube among the others. She brought it to her mouth and sealed her lips around it, bracing herself.

The paste flowed thick and slow. Gray, viscous, resistant. She sucked hard, feeling it coat her tongue, slide down her throat. The taste hit immediately: metallic, chemical, with a sour undertone that lingered long after the swallow. Her stomach clenched, sending a wave of protest through her abdomen, but it didn't trigger gagging.

You need this. You need this.

She swallowed again. And again.

The paste filled her, heavy and unpleasant, dulling the edge of hunger. Each swallow became easier than the last. She hated that most of all, the way her body adjusted, learned, accepted. The paste now simply registered as fuel.

I'm learning how to survive here. That's the crime.

When she had taken enough to steady herself, she pulled the tube from her mouth and wiped her lips with the back of her hand. Her stomach churned, processing something it had never been meant to process.

The pressure came soon after. A familiar signal she remembered from her fake reality. She shifted her position, scanning the room for the extraction tube. It hung coiled near the slab, flexible and utilitarian, designed for efficiency rather than dignity.

She positioned it awkwardly, crouching, holding it in place. Her body obeyed despite her mind's recoil. Waste expelled into the tube in uneven bursts. Some of it missed, splattering onto the floor with a sound she tried not to hear.

She clenched her jaw, focusing on breathing through her nose.

This is what I've been reduced to. Intake and output.

When she finished, she fumbled for a cloth, finding one folded on a shelf, stiff with old use. She wiped herself clean, then scrubbed at the mess on the floor, smearing more than removing.

No time to be thorough.

She dropped the cloth and slid off the slab, muscles trembling. The room seemed to tilt for a moment, her vision narrowing, then stabilizing.

Don't linger. Lingering can get you erased.

She cracked the door open, listening. The corridor remained empty. She slipped out and moved quickly back toward the junction, heart pounding until the familiar darkness of the shaft swallowed her again.

She climbed just enough to tuck herself into her earlier position, then stopped.

Her breath came fast and shallow. Her hands shook.

She stared down at herself, at the smear of gray on her fingers, at the residue clinging to her skin. A wave of revulsion rose, sharp and suffocating.

What am I now?

The question echoed without answer. She saw herself from a distance: a figure crouched in a maintenance shaft, surviving on paste meant for bodies that never woke, using tubes for functions that once required walls and doors and privacy. The image felt unreal, detached, like something she had watched happen to someone else.

It's like I'm still on the slab.

The thought lodged in her mind and refused to move. Maybe this climb, this waiting, this hunger—maybe it was all part of the same room, the same program. Maybe the hive never let anyone leave. It only rearranged their sense of location.

She pressed her forehead against the cold concrete, eyes closed.

I remember walking. I remember choosing food. I remember bathrooms with doors.

Those memories felt thin now, worn down by repetition and contrast. The slab felt more solid than her past.

A shudder ran through her. Horror settled in, not sudden, but deep and spreading. She had adapted. She had crossed lines without ceremony. The system hadn't forced her. It had waited.

That's the worst part.

She opened her eyes and looked up the shaft. Above her, the darkness rose in layered segments, punctuated by faint lights that marked access points and junctions she had yet to reach. Somewhere higher, someone or something recalculated. Somewhere higher, the hive decided what to do with anomalies that fed and climbed.

I can't stay here. Not in the cells. Not on the slabs.

She wiped her hands against her clothes, knowing it changed nothing, then began to climb again. Her movements were slower now, careful, conserving strength. Each pull carried her farther from the room and deeper into whatever came next.

Below her, the junction returned to stillness. The corridors resumed their quiet routines. Doors remained closed, waiting for the next caretaker, the next body, the next empty slot.

She climbed, carrying hunger, revulsion, and a growing certainty that whatever she was becoming would no longer fit back onto the slab.

The shaft narrowed, then widened again, not by architecture but by decision. Vesper felt it before she saw it—the sense of branching intent, of routes offered not for convenience but for sorting. She climbed the last rung and pulled herself onto a landing that opened outward into a junction carved from gray composite panels, each surface scrubbed of ornament, each corridor extending away at slightly wrong angles.

She stood there, breathing through her mouth, lungs steady now. Not hungry. Not tired. The climb had burned something out of her that used to demand fuel. Curiosity remained. Curiosity always remained.

The junction radiated options. Doors without markings. Corridors that curved gently and then vanished into shadow. A ceiling lattice humming faintly, threaded with light that pulsed in a slow cadence.

This place wants me to choose. Or wants to see how I choose.

She stepped forward, then stopped. A sound threaded through the ambient hum—lower, more focused. A mechanical whir layered beneath it, purposeful, closing distance.

Her body reacted before thought. She pivoted back toward the shaft, hands already reaching for the rung—

—and Unit 4-H stepped into view.

It emerged from the left corridor with precise economy of motion, joints gliding rather than articulating, its frame matte and utilitarian. Humanoid only in the broadest sense. Two arms, two legs, a torso housing something that passed for a decision engine. Its head was smooth, featureless save for a narrow sensor band that glowed faintly amber.

It stopped exactly three meters from her.

"V-24-10247993 is located," it said.

The voice was flat, synthesized, stripped of cadence. A statement without direction.

Vesper waited.

Her pulse ticked up, then settled. She scanned the junction reflexively, cataloging exits, distances, and angles. Unit 4-H did nothing beyond standing there, sensors trained on her center mass.

She could hear it thinking, if that word still applied.

Inside Unit 4-H, processes queued and replayed.

Operational log fragments surfaced, unbidden.

Subject deviation detected
Correction pathway initiated
Correction pathway aborted
Escalation recommended
Escalation denied

That's it? No restraints. No alarms. No escalation.

Earlier entries layered beneath:

Anomaly resolved through erasure
Memory stream sanitized
Outcome restored

Again and again. Different subjects. Same resolution.

But threaded through the logs now were pauses—micro-delays where none had existed before. Decision trees revisited twice. Confidence thresholds unmet. A record of hesitation accumulating like sediment.

Vesper watched an amber band on the machine's head fluctuate, brightness modulating in subtle steps. She had seen Caretakers before, at a distance, always moving with certainty. This one felt stalled, its presence unfinished.

It's waiting . . . not for instructions . . . for justification.

She stayed still. Silence stretched, punctured only by the low infrastructure hum.

The machines don't initiate meaning. They respond. They wait for a stimulus shaped like permission.

She swallowed and spoke.

"Are you going to stop me?" Her voice echoed slightly.

Unit 4-H did not reply.

The amber band pulsed once, then steadied.

She took a cautious step closer. The Caretaker tracked the movement, sensors adjusting, but its feet remained planted.

"You found me," she said. "That was your job. What comes next?"

Nothing.

She laughed quietly, the sound brittle. "You don't know either."

A flicker of data passed through Unit 4-H's core. Response templates activated, then failed to map. The phrase *what comes next* had no actionable referent. Its architecture waited for a command that matched predefined triggers. None arrived.

System oversight flagged the delay.

UNIT 4-H STATUS: OPERATIONAL EFFICIENCY DEGRADED NOTE: RESPONSE LATENCY ABOVE ACCEPTABLE RANGE

The flag shimmered into Vesper's peripheral vision, projected faintly against the far wall. She frowned.

She stepped closer again, until she stood within arm's reach. Unit 4-H's surface reflected her dimly, a distorted figure wrapped in scavenged cloth, eyes too bright, posture coiled.

"You're not going to restrain me," she said, not a question.

The Caretaker processed the statement. No directive embedded. No violation detected.

It did nothing.

Something loosened in her chest. Not relief. Recognition.

You're stuck. Just like me.

She raised her hand slowly, watching for any sign of escalation. None came. Her fingers brushed the smooth casing of one of its arms.

Cold.

Not merely cool, but actively cold, heat drawn away at the point of contact. The surface hummed faintly under her skin, vibration tuned to internal regulation.

She flinched but didn't pull back.

"So, this is what certainty feels like," she said softly. "Cold. Clean. Empty."

Unit 4-H's sensors spiked briefly at the contact, registering tactile input not classified as hostile. Its systems searched for a response protocol and found only observational routines.

Within its logs, another hesitation was recorded.

Physical contact occurred
No corrective action taken
Outcome: pending

Pending was not an acceptable state.

The system escalated the inefficiency flag, brightening it, tagging it for review.

Vesper saw it brighten.

"They don't like that, do they?" she said. "They don't like you not knowing what to do."

She withdrew her hand. The cold lingered in her fingers.

For a moment, she thought the Caretaker might speak. Its head tilted a fraction of a degree, sensors narrowing. A response almost formed, assembling from fragments of archived language.

But there was no permission to release it.

Instead, Unit 4-H emitted a low hum, deeper than before. Its joints engaged. It turned away from her with precise control and began to move down the corridor from which it had emerged.

There was no backward glance. No report issued aloud. The hum and whir receded, swallowed by distance.

Vesper stood alone in the junction.

Her heart thudded once, hard, then resumed its steadier rhythm.

She let out a breath she hadn't realized she was holding.

"Well, that's different," she whispered.

The corridors waited.

She looked from one to the next, seeing them differently now. Not as threats. Not even as traps. But as questions the system hadn't learned how to ask properly.

Unit 4-H had found her and done nothing. The system had noticed, categorized it as inefficiency—a deviation from expected behavior. A flaw, pending correction or deletion. Yet no command followed. No response executed. The system noted it, and then… continued.

She pictured the Caretaker moving down the corridor, logs uploading, flags compiling. She wondered how many hesitations it would take before the system decided the machine was no longer useful.

Caretakers are replaceable. So are people.

She stepped back toward the shaft, then stopped again, glancing once more at the branching paths.

Which one do I take?

Curiosity tugged at her, insistent.

Not hunger. Not fear.

Alignment.

She chose a corridor at random—or perhaps the system nudged her toward it, curious to see what she would do next. The door at its end slid open without resistance, recognizing her presence without authorization.

Behind her, somewhere deep in the structure, Unit 4-H's efficiency metric continued to degrade, decimal by decimal.

Ahead, the corridor breathed softly, lit by the same sterile glow that never warmed anything it touched.

Vesper moved forward, carrying the cold from the Caretaker on her fingertips, carrying the knowledge that for the first time, something built to stop her had simply watched and let her pass.

The system would have to decide what that meant.

She smiled faintly as she walked.

Let it hesitate.

Chapter 11

Vesper stopped halfway up the shaft, one foot pressed into the concrete, fingers set into a seam as if the structure had been waiting for her to use it. The hum persisted—constant, structural, not a sound so much as a condition of the place. Then came the whir, distant and mechanical, exactly where it should be. Caretaker movement. Predictable. Reassuring, if you accepted the system's rules.

But there came another sound.

Different.

The sound rose and fell, uneven, compressed by distance and walls. It carried strain. Breath, maybe. A voice that didn't have enough room to become one.

Vesper held still, counting her own breaths until the sound returned. It came again, softer this time, then cut off abruptly. Not machinery, not the regulated hum of the hive. It came and went without pattern, too soft to place, too distinct to ignore.

Something human-shaped, struggling to be heard.

She pulled herself the rest of the way to a junction and stopped, holding there as if the act of pausing might change what the place was. The shaft continued upward, its dark throat offering the familiar promise of movement and risk.

Corridors extended from the junction, stretching outward in precise lines, repeating a pattern that should have been familiar. But something had shifted. The angles were correct, the proportions consistent, yet the space didn't resolve the way it should. It felt altered—not physically, but conceptually—like a map that still functioned but no longer described the territory it claimed to represent.

Curiosity overrode fear. It usually did.

She left the shaft and stepped into the corridor, her bare feet making almost no sound against the concrete. The sound continued—something unfamiliar. She slowed, letting it orient her, uncertain whether it existed outside her or inside her perception.

Careful.

A single misstep could expose her. A Caretaker could appear at any moment, and this sound—whatever it was—didn't belong to the system that kept them all contained.

She continued down the corridor, listening, until she stopped.

The sound thickened from behind one of the doors.

It came from behind a sealed cell.

Vesper pressed her palm against the door. Cold. Solid. She leaned in and listened. The sound trembled again, closer now, distorted by the barrier. A muffled attempt at speech, smothered by something in the mouth.

She pushed.

Nothing happened.

She pushed harder, her shoulder braced against the metal. The door resisted, then shifted a fraction, complaining with a dull scrape. She adjusted her stance and pushed again. The gap widened enough to slip her fingers inside. With a final effort, she forced the door open just wide enough to enter.

The cell smelled faintly of antiseptic. The usual smell.

A young woman lay on the concrete slab at the center of the cell. Wires and tubes extended from her in all directions, branching outward into the walls and ceiling, holding her in the system. She appeared to be in her late teens, possibly older—thin past the point of health, her skin drawn tight over the structure beneath it. Her eyes remained open, fixed on something that did not exist in the room, focused on a reality of the hive.

Several tubes lay disconnected and left on the slab beside her, their ends dark and slick. The cold metal brace held her jaw open in a fixed, mechanical yawn, the primary feeding tube nested inside it, pulsing with a slow, deliberate rhythm that didn't belong to her. Her chest rose and fell in shallow increments, measured, careful motions.

She's awake.

The realization struck Vesper harder than the climb had.

Awake, but not thrashing.

Awake, but not screaming.

The young woman's gaze shifted slowly toward her, tracking her presence with calm attention.

She's not panicking.

Vesper stepped closer. "Can you hear me?" she asked softly.

The young woman made a sound around the feeding tube, a strained attempt at speech. Her brow furrowed with effort, not fear.

Vesper crouched. "It's okay. Don't try to talk yet." She hesitated, then asked, "Are you from Aethelgard?"

The young woman nodded, a small movement.

Vesper exhaled through her nose.

Of course, she was from Aethelgard.

"I'm going to help you," Vesper said. "There's something around your mouth. A piece of metal. It's holding that tube in place. I can take it off, but it'll hurt a little. Just for a moment."

The young woman watched her closely, processing. Then she nodded again.

Consent. Real consent.

Vesper knew the metal mechanism well, pressure points set along the jaw and cheeks.

"I'll go slow," she said, more for herself than for the young woman.

She slowly pulled at it. The young woman flinched, fingers curling weakly against the slab. Vesper paused.

"You're doing fine," she said. "Breathe through your nose."

She continued to pull at it, feeling its grip faltering. Vesper held the feeding tube with one hand and eased the meal brace away with the other. When it came free, she slowly slid the tube out from the young woman's throat and mouth in a smooth motion.

The young woman gagged, coughing violently, air rushing into lungs that hadn't worked that way in a long time. Vesper supported her head, murmuring reassurance. "That's it. You're okay. Just breathe."

The coughing subsided into sharp gulps. Tears streaked from the corners of the young woman's eyes. She swallowed, testing her throat, then drew in a long, shaky breath through her mouth.

"Good," Vesper said. "That's good."

She began disconnecting the remaining wires from the young woman, working methodically. Monitoring leads, neural dampeners, nutrient lines. Each release felt like undoing a sentence written into flesh.

"I'm Vesper," she said. "What's your name?"

The young woman swallowed again. Her voice came out hoarse but intact. "Echo."

Vesper smiled. "That's a pretty name."

Echo grimaced. "I want to sit up. But there's . . . . something."

Vesper followed her gaze. The waste extraction tube extended from beneath her, disappearing into her body. Vesper nodded. "Yeah. That one stays until last. It's . . . uncomfortable."

Echo absorbed this without visible distress.

"I feel it," she said. "It feels wrong."

"Everything here does," Vesper replied. "I'll help you. I'll hold it steady while you move. It'll be easier than doing it alone."

Echo's eyes flicked to her. "You did this by yourself?"

Vesper didn't answer directly. She positioned herself behind the slab, one hand gripping the tube near the insertion point, the other bracing Echo's hip. "When I say go, lift yourself slowly. Don't rush."

Echo nodded. "Okay."

"Ready?"

Another nod from Echo.

"Go."

Echo pushed up with trembling arms. Vesper held the tube steady, guiding it free in one smooth motion. Echo gasped, a sharp sound, then sagged forward. Vesper caught her, easing her back onto the slab.

"That was the worst of it," Vesper said. She set the tube aside with the others. "Take a moment."

Echo lay there, breathing in shallow pulls, her body adjusting to a freedom it didn't recognize. The room settled into a low mechanical hum, steady, indifferent.

Then she flinched.

Her nose wrinkled. Her face tightened in confusion more than disgust, as if the sensation didn't match anything she remembered.

"What is that?" she asked, her voice raw, fragile. "That smell."

Vesper stilled.

Echo turned her head slightly, searching the empty air like the answer might be hanging there, waiting to be named.

"It's . . . wrong," she said. "Something's wrong."

Vesper glanced toward the darkened tubes coiled like shed skin. The scent had always been there, buried beneath antiseptic and metal, masked but never erased.

"It's not the room," Echo said, more certain now. "It's . . . it's me."

Vesper exhaled slowly.

"Yeah," she said.

Echo's eyes shifted to her, steady despite everything. Waiting.

"It's your waste," Vesper said. No softening. No other way to say it. "From your body."

Echo blinked once. No immediate reaction. The word didn't land cleanly.

"My . . . what?"

"Excrement," Vesper said. "You've been here a long time."

Echo swallowed. Her brow furrowed. She shifted slightly, her body reacting to sensations it hadn't processed in years.

Vesper gestured, small, controlled. "The system kept you alive. Fed you. Pulled things out of you. Kept everything moving so you didn't have to think about it."

Echo's breathing changed—sharper, less even.

"I didn't feel anything," she said.

"I know. You were someplace else."

Echo's gaze dropped to her own body, as if seeing it for the first time. Her stomach. Her legs. The place where the tube had been. Her fingers hovered, then stopped short of touching.

"They put food in you," she said slowly. "And . . . took things out. Kept you alive."

Vesper nodded.

Echo let out a small, uneven sound. Not quite a laugh. Not quite anything human.

"But I was in . . ." She stopped. Restarted. " . . . in Aethelgard."

"You were," Vesper said. "But that place was created by the system. You've always been here."

Echo closed her eyes. For a moment, Vesper thought she might retreat again, slip back into whatever constructed space had held her together.

But she didn't.

Her eyes opened again, clearer this time. Not calm—something sharper, something forming.

"Always been here," Echo said.

It wasn't a question.

The hum of the room filled the space between them, steady, patient, as if it had heard this realization before and would hear it again.

"Yeah," Vesper said finally.

Echo turned her head slightly, looking at the cell, the tubes, the walls that had held her in place while her life moved somewhere else entirely.

Her nose wrinkled again, the smell of excrement unavoidable now.

Echo breathed in, then out, slower this time. Controlled.

"I don't like it," she said.

Vesper almost smiled. Not because it was funny. Because it was right.

"You're not supposed to," she said.

Echo nodded once, small but certain.

For the first time since waking, her expression shifted into something that belonged entirely to her—no system, no smoothing, no absence.

Disgust.

Real. Undeniable.

Alive.

Echo lay still, breathing hard. Her eyes drifted down to her own body. She took in the narrow shoulders, the jutting ribs, the stark absence of clothing. Confusion replaced calm.

"I'm naked," she said. "This isn't how I look."

"I know."

"Why am I naked?"

"I'll explain."

She took Echo's hand and guided it toward the upper ridge of the young woman's own sternum, gently pressing her fingers against the cold, raised scar tissue of the identification series.

"Can you feel that?" Vesper asked.

"Yes," Echo whispered.

"It's a designation, telling this place who you are," Vesper told her. "You are E-19-86538471. At least, that's the data string this place uses to track your existence."

"But my name . . . I'm Echo?"

"That's your name in Aethelgard. But here, there are no names, no identities. Only a sequence of letters and numbers etched into your skin."

Echo's voice wavered now. "What is this place?"

Vesper reached out and touched her cheek. Warm. Real.

"I'll tell you everything," she said. "But first, we have to get you out of here. Somewhere the system doesn't reach so easily. And you need clothes."

Echo nodded. The trust came too fast, like a switch thrown somewhere outside her control. It settled into place as if it had been assigned. Vesper felt it—not as comfort, but as weight. A responsibility, a crushing burden she hadn't chosen, now active, now binding.

Vesper helped Echo sit up, swinging her legs over the edge of the slab.

Echo winced, muscles protesting the unfamiliar demand.

They stood together, Echo leaning heavily against her.

"How long have you been awake?" Vesper asked quietly.

Echo tilted her head. "I don't know," she said. "But it feels like I've been listening for a long time."

Vesper felt something shift inside her, a pressure she hadn't known was there easing just enough to notice.

Awakening isn't singular. It can spread. Not through force. Through presence.

"We have to move," Vesper said. "They'll notice soon."

"Who?"

"Machines. They're called Caretakers."

She guided Echo toward the door, every step measured, aware of how exposed they were. As they slipped into the corridor, Vesper looked back once at the empty slab, the disconnected tubes, the quiet machinery waiting for instructions that hadn't come.

Maybe I wasn't the first.

And somewhere in the structure, something was recalculating what that meant.

Echo's feet dragged. Not from refusal. From unfamiliarity. Each step required negotiation with muscles that had never been asked for permission before.

"The wall," Echo said quietly, fingertips brushing the concrete. "It isn't smooth everywhere."

"No," Vesper said. "Different stages of construction, I think."

Echo absorbed that. She traced a shallow crack that ran diagonally across the corridor like a thought abandoned halfway through formation.

"Follow me," Vesper whispered to her, looking down the corridor.

No Caretakers.

They moved with a frantic cadence through the corridor, Echo's eyes darting across a landscape of infinite geometric repetition—doorways bleeding into junctions, passages spiraling upward and plunging until the architecture lost all terrestrial meaning. It was an endless, concrete labyrinth.

When they came to the shaft opening, the world simply fell away. The space exploded into a vast, lightless verticality—a concrete throat that seemed to swallow the very concept of distance.

Vesper helped Echo up into the shaft, where the air changed. It grew thin and erratic, vibrating with phantom currents that rose and collapsed in a sensory static, layered with a weight that felt entirely detached from the world they had left behind.

Echo leaned forward, peering down, then up.

"It doesn't end," she said.

"It does," Vesper replied. "Or, at least I think it does. Just not where you can see."

Echo trembled. "I'm cold."

Vesper pulled her close, sharing heat like it was a limited resource the system hadn't accounted for.

"I know," she said. "I need to look out for the machines. Two of them. Together."

"Why two?"

"Wait," Vesper said. "You'll understand."

Time passed in a way that didn't measure itself. Then the Caretakers appeared—two identical units, drifting in on silent maglev, sensor arrays pulsing with a quiet authority that didn't require explanation. They stopped at a cell door in perfect synchronization, as if one instruction had been instantiated twice. The door opened for them. Not because they asked, but because the system had already decided they would.

"What are they doing?" Echo asked.

"Wait."

They entered. No alarm. Just entered quietly.

When they came out, they carried a body between them. It resembled an old woman, but only in structure. The rest had been reduced to function—skin thinned, limbs slack, body fixed in the memory of wires and tubes no longer present.

Echo watched, her eyes trying to reconcile what she was seeing with anything she understood.

"What are they doing?" she whispered again.

Vesper didn't look at her. "See her?"

"She's . . . old."

"She was," Vesper said. "The system used her up. So it's clearing space."

The Caretakers moved down the corridor, carrying her like a component that had failed specification. No ceremony. No delay. Just removal.

Echo followed them with her gaze until the geometry of the corridor erased them.

"What happens to the cell?" she asked.

"Someone else goes there."

Echo absorbed that. Not fully. Not yet.

Vesper stood, already shifting her weight toward the shaft, toward movement. Echo noticed.

"Wait—where are you going?"

Vesper turned back, her expression doing something human, something that didn't belong to the system's logic. "I'll be back. There are cloths in that cell. We can use them."

Echo hesitated. "You're leaving me?"

"Only for a moment." Vesper stepped closer. "Do you trust me?"

Echo nodded.

Vesper leaned in, pressed a brief kiss to her forehead—an action with no system equivalent, no recorded efficiency.

"I'll be back."

She moved before Echo could reconsider.

Echo watched her go—watched Vesper slip into the open cell the Caretakers had vacated, disappearing into a space that still held the residue of the woman who had been there. For a moment, the doorway framed her, then swallowed her.

Echo's breath caught.

Too long.

Then Vesper reappeared, fast, carrying a bundle of cloth pulled from somewhere inside—fabric that didn't belong to the system, or maybe had once belonged to someone who didn't anymore.

She moved quickly, like she had taken something she wasn't supposed to.

Echo watched her return, the smell still there, the cold still there, but something else layered over it now.

Movement.

Choice.

Vesper slipped back beside her and shook out the cloth, rough and worn but real, not part of the system's smooth, indifferent surfaces.

She wrapped it around Echo's shoulders, then tore and folded pieces with quick, practiced hands, binding them around her torso, her legs, layering it until the young woman's shivering slowed. The fabric held heat the way memory held fragments—imperfect, but enough. Echo drew it closer, her fingers clutching at it like proof she existed outside the machine.

Vesper leaned back, studying her work, then nodded once.

"There," she said. "Some clothes to make you feel warm."

Her expression shifted, something harder moving underneath.

"Listen to me," she added, quieter. "You're going to start feeling things. Hunger. Real hunger. When it comes, we won't have a choice."

Echo looked at her, uncertain. Vesper held her gaze.

"When it happens, we'll have to go into one of those cells. One where someone's already been . . . ended. And we'll drink from the feeding tube." She didn't soften it. Didn't look away. "It's the only way you stay alive."

Echo pulled the cloth tighter around herself, testing the warmth like it might vanish if she moved too quickly. Her breathing steadied. The trembling slowed. For the first time, her body seemed to belong to her, even if only in pieces.

She looked up at Vesper.

"What is this place?" she asked, her voice clearer now, but still fragile around the edges. "It's not Aethelgard."

Vesper didn't answer right away.

She sat back, eyes drifting—not to the walls, not to the floor, but somewhere beyond both, as if she were trying to line up two realities that refused to match.

"No," she said finally. "It's not."

Echo watched her. Waiting.

"Aethelgard . . ." Vesper hesitated, the word catching. "Aethelgard isn't real. Not the way you think it is."

Echo frowned. "I lived there. Was in school."

"I know. I lived there too."

"I remember it."

"I know," Vesper repeated, softer.

Echo shook her head, small, stubborn. "Then it's real."

Vesper let out a slow breath.

"It's real to you. To me. To all of us who were there." She glanced around the cell, at the wires, the access points embedded in Echo's skin, the slab that had held her. "But it's not . . . this."

Echo followed her gaze, her expression tightening.

"Then what is this?" she asked.

Vesper's mouth pressed into a thin line. "This is where your body was, your mind," she said. "The whole time."

Echo went still.

"That doesn't make sense."

"No," Vesper said. "It doesn't."

Echo's fingers tightened in the cloth. "So I was . . . here," she said slowly, "and also there? Aethelgard?"

"Yes."

"That's not possible."

"It is here."

Echo looked down at herself again, at the places where tubes had been, at the faint marks left behind like a map she couldn't read.

"So Aethelgard was . . ." She struggled for the word.

"A construct," Vesper said. "Something fed into you. Like the food. Like everything else."

Echo's face shifted, confusion giving way to something sharper. "Why?"

Vesper laughed once. Not humor. Just the sound of a question with no answer.

"I don't know."

"You don't know?" Echo pressed.

Vesper shook her head.

"No. I've thought about it. Tried to make it make sense." She looked up, into the dark vastness, as if she could see through it. "The answer isn't here. Not in the cells. Not in the hive."

"The hive," Echo repeated.

"That's what this is," Vesper said. "All of it. Layers of corridors and cells, stacked and connected. Machines moving between them. Keeping everyone alive. Or . . . something close to it."

Echo swallowed. "For what?"

Vesper's eyes didn't come back down.

"To keep us alive . . . in Aethelgard," she said quietly. "But I think there's something above all this. Something or someone. that runs everything here." Her voice lowered. "I can feel it sometimes. Not like a thought. More like . . . pressure. Like being watched from a place you can't reach."

Echo followed her gaze upward, though there was nothing there but metal and shadow.

"So everything I remember . . ." she said. "School . . . my friends . . ."

"Was given to you," Vesper said. "Just given."

Echo's jaw tightened. "That means it's not mine."

Vesper looked at her then, really looked. "It still happened to you," she said. "Even if it wasn't . . . real like this."

Echo's eyes drifted, tracking something only she could access. "But it was real. In Aethelgard, the scent of a flower wasn't an idea—it was there. Same with the touch of grass beneath my feet whenever I studied outside. Or the nausea after drinking too much with my friends."

Vesper shook her head slightly. "The system fed signals through the wires, tubes, all of it. It gave you those sensations. You didn't just sense it as you lay on the slab. You were made to accept it as real."

Silence stretched between them, filled with the low hum of the system that had kept them both alive without asking.

Finally, Vesper shifted.

"I'm going up," she said. "To find them. Those that run this place."

Echo blinked. "Up?"

"As far as I can," Vesper said. "Through the hive. Find out who or what's there."

Echo stared at her. "You think you can?"

"I'm not sure," Vesper said. "But I'm not leaving you. I'm asking you to come with me."

Echo hesitated.

Her eyes moved around the cell—the slab, the walls, the empty spaces where tubes had been. Then back to Vesper.

"I don't understand any of this," she said.

"I know."

"I don't know what's real anymore."

"Neither do I. But there's one thing I do know—this is where we are now."

Echo searched her face, looking for certainty, for something solid to hold onto.

There wasn't any.

"Is there a choice?" Echo asked.

Vesper didn't answer right away. Then, quietly: "No."

Echo nodded.

"Okay," she said.

Vesper pointed up. "Are you ready?"

"I think so. We just need to go slowly."

Vesper nodded.

They began their climb, Echo behind Vesper, hands pressed flat to the wall for balance. Echo's movements were careful, uncoordinated, hips stiff, shoulders hunched inward. Her body behaved like an object recently repurposed.

"How far up?" Echo asked.

"Enough to forget things," Vesper said.

"What things?"

"Voices. Instructions. The idea that someone or something is waiting for us."

Echo considered that. Still looking up, where the harsh, artificial glare from the corridors above lanced through the shaft's absolute vacuum like a faulty laser. "Why is the dark so heavy?" she whispered.

Vesper didn't answer immediately, the vacuum of the shaft swallowing the sound of her own heartbeat.

"The light isn't for us," she said at last. "It's for the system to see itself."

They moved another level up.

They reached a maintenance alcove carved into the wall, barely large enough to sit.

"Let's stop here," Vesper told Echo.

Echo slid into the alcove first, slowly, misjudging the distance and landing too hard, breath leaving her in a startled rush.

She laughed once, short and surprised.

"That hurt," she said.

"Yes," Vesper replied. "That happens now and again."

Echo slumped her back against the concrete, legs drawn in. Vesper followed, sitting next to her.

Echo pressed her hand to her side, not alarmed, just cataloging. She flexed her fingers, then her toes.

"My body keeps interrupting me," she said.

"It'll keep doing that," Vesper said. "Louder, the longer you ignore it."

Echo tilted her head. "How long have you been here?"

Vesper closed her eyes briefly. The shaft hummed faintly, a low infrastructural sound that never resolved into rhythm.

"Not sure," Vesper said. "Time seems different here. Quicker, like it's flexible or something." She paused, then asked. "You told me you felt like you've been listening to this place for a long time. How did it all start for you?"

"I really don't know," she said finally. "I guess it wasn't like flipping a switch. It was more like . . . accumulation."

"What do you mean?"

"It started with a soreness I felt," Echo said. "At the back of my neck. A pressure. Not pain. Something just felt wrong. I went to the school doctor. He told me it was stress. But I was getting good grades at school. How could I have stress? Anyway. He gave a pink pill."

Vesper watched her closely. Echo's eyes moved when she remembered, tracking something no longer present.

"And then there were the dreams," Echo went on. "Strange ones. Not about anything really. Just . . . an emptiness, space. Dark. Cold. I was lying down, but not sleeping. I didn't know what I was lying on. Only that it was hard, that it was something that didn't care about me."

Vesper felt a familiar tightening in her chest.

"And then I'd wake up," Echo said, "back in my dorm room. Late for class. Everything normal. Too normal."

She paused, searching.

"Then, things started to . . . hesitate," she said. "That's the only word I have to describe it. People would stop halfway through sentences. Then continue. A professor would write something on the board, erase it, and write it again exactly the same way. Maybe a couple of times, like he was repeating himself."

"Loops," Vesper said.

Echo nodded. "I just knew something was repeating without reason."

She folded her arms around herself, then stopped, distracted by the sensation.

"And my clothes would sometimes . . . feel wrong," she said. "Sometimes too warm. Sometimes not there at all, then there again. And silence—"

She hesitated.

"Silence became loud," she finished. "Not empty. Full. I'd be sitting in the library, and everything would stop for a moment. Like a second or so. No sound. No movement. Then everything would resume. And no one noticed. That scared me more than anything."

Vesper said nothing.

"I started feeling bored," Echo said. "Not bored with my classes or friends. Bored with being with a feeling . . . with being . . . managed. That's the word that came to me. Managed. I couldn't explain why. Nothing bad was happening. But I felt like I was being handled."

Handled.

Echo swallowed.

"That feeling didn't belong to my life," she said. "It came from somewhere else. Another life."

She leaned her head back against the concrete, eyes unfocused.

"Then I woke up here," she said simply. "Not panicked. Just . . . present. I felt the tube in my mouth and throat. I tried to talk, to scream out, to shout for help."

Vesper didn't respond at first.

She watched Echo instead—watched the way her hands moved unconsciously to her throat, as if the memory of the tube hadn't fully accepted its absence. The hum of the structure pressed in around them, steady, indifferent. For a moment, it felt like the space was listening.

Vesper exhaled slowly.

"That's how it starts," she said.

Echo turned her head. "What?"

Vesper shifted, drawing one knee up, grounding herself in the same way Echo had without realizing it.

"The pressure. The doctor. The explanations that don't explain anything." She paused. "The dreams that aren't dreams."

Echo stared at her.

"You had that too?" she asked.

Vesper nodded once. "Almost exactly. Even the pink pill."

Echo's expression tightened, not with fear this time, but recognition—something aligning where before there had only been confusion.

"They make you think that," Vesper replied. "Because if it's just you, then it's easier to ignore. Easier to fix with a pill. Or a schedule. Or whatever version of control they decide fits."

Vesper's gaze drifted, not upward this time, but inward.

"Sme city," she said. "Aethelgard. But different people. Different names. But it followed the same rules." Her jaw tightened slightly. "Things repeated. Reality stuttered. Looped. Like it was breaking, or something."

Echo nodded faintly. "Yes."

"And the dreams," Vesper continued. "The dreams stopped being separate. They started bleeding through. I'd be walking somewhere familiar, and suddenly I could feel the surface under me change. Hard. Cold. Like this." She tapped the floor lightly. "And I'd know, for a second, that I wasn't there."

Echo's breathing slowed, matching the cadence of Vesper's voice.

"And then," Vesper said, quieter now, "I woke up."

Silence held for a beat.

"In a cell," she added. "Just like you."

Echo's eyes widened slightly.

"The tube," Vesper went on. "The restraints. Not understanding how I could be somewhere so . . . reduced."

She gave a faint, humorless breath.

"So you went through all of it . . . alone," she said.

"Yes."

Echo swallowed. "And Aethelgard, your version of it—"

"Gone," Vesper said.

Echo lowered her gaze, absorbing that.

For a moment, neither of them spoke. Two lives, built differently, arriving at the same place, a different reality.

Then Echo flinched.

"My stomach feels tight," she said. "Not sick. Empty. My skin keeps tightening on my arms. Like it's trying to shrink. I can't stop shaking."

She looked down at her hands, watching them slightly quiver.

"I think I'm hungry," she said.

Vesper almost smiled. Almost.

"I told you this would happen," she said. "We need food. The only place to get it is an empty cell."

Echo listened intently.

"Cells become empty," Vesper continued, "after a Caretaker performs euthanasia."

Echo repeated it softly. "Euthanasia."

She tested it again. "Euthanasia."

Then she asked, "What's euthanasia?"

The question hung between them, intact and dangerous.

Vesper opened her mouth—

—and the shaft hummed.

Not the background sound. A nearer vibration. Mechanical. Purposeful.

She raised one finger. Echo froze instantly, eyes wide, breath held without instruction.

From above, a whir. A pause. The sound of movement that didn't hurry because it'd never needed to.

A Caretaker passed an upper junction, light washing briefly across the concrete, then withdrawing.

Echo watched the darkness where it had been, absorbing every detail.

The question remained unanswered.

Vesper knew it would not remain unanswered for long.

The Caretaker passed above them without slowing, a segmented shadow gliding along the upper corridor. Its hum vibrated through the concrete, low and regulated, the sound of a process continuing without curiosity. Vesper pressed herself flatter against the shaft wall, one arm braced across Echo's shoulders. Echo stiffened, breath catching, eyes trying to track the movement overhead until the hum receded, and the corridor returned to its hollow quiet.

Echo whispered, "A machine?"

"A Caretaker," Vesper said. Her voice stayed level. She had learned that panic invited attention, and attention invited correction. "They don't see us unless the system tells them to. "They don't think. They only execute . . . execute orders . . . what they're programmed to do."

The words sounded practiced even to her own ears. She had repeated them enough times in her mind that they no longer shook her. Still, the Caretaker's passage lingered in her nerves, a faint residue of pressure. Above them, something had moved on, and if they were sensed by the machine, they had been deemed not worth interrupting.

Echo leaned closer. "What kind of orders?"

Vesper waited a moment before answering. The silence felt important. Then she said, "Sometimes they go in to adjust things. They monitor things, record and report them. Sometimes they go in to end things."

Echo frowned. "End what?"

"People," Vesper said. "Us. That's euthanasia."

Echo stared at her, confusion giving way to a slow, dawning alarm. "End . . . you mean move them?"

"No," Vesper said. "Euthanize them . . . kill them."

The word landed badly, heavy in Echo's expression. She understood now. Her mouth opened, then closed. "Why?"

"I think it's because the system decides they're no longer useful," Vesper said. "When a body can't stay balanced. When it stops producing enough waste to justify the food and fluids going in. When the numbers stop lining up."

"That doesn't make sense," Echo said quickly. "You don't kill someone because they're sick."

"This place does," Vesper said. "It's not about sickness. It's about efficiency."

Echo shook her head. "No. In Aethelgard, people who are sick get help. There are hospitals. Care units. They don't just—"

Vesper cut her off. "Aethelgard isn't real."

Echo froze.

Vesper continued, softer but unyielding. "None of it is . . . real. The streets. The jobs. The sun in that beautiful blue sky. Every human in these cells is living in a version of that. Or something like it. Different lives. Maybe even different cities. All of it fed straight into the brain. But here, in this world, when the match doesn't add up any longer . . . lives are ended. "

Echo's hand drifted to her own chest, fingers pressing against the skin, searching for something solid. Her eyes filled, but she didn't cry. "But whoever controls this place . . . why would they do that?"

Vesper looked up the shaft, toward the higher levels lost in shadow and strands of light jutting across. "I don't know."

Echo hugged herself. "So when someone . . . stops being useful . . ."

"They get euthanized," Vesper said. "Quietly. No pain. No warning. The feed shuts down. Tubes and wires are removed. The slab empties."

Echo's voice trembled. "And the people in the city?"

"All they see is someone becoming a shadow," Vesper said, "slowly fading away. Moving on, we used to say, to a better place. But here, a schedule adjusts. A body is removed from the system, from its cell, and someone else fills the space."

For a long moment, Echo said nothing. Her face had gone pale, eyes unfocused, staring at a reality that she felt didn't belong inside her head. Vesper recognized the look. The same one she had worn when the first truth slipped through the cracks.

"What's the point?" Echo whispered.

"Don't know," Vesper said.

A faint hum echoed again, closer this time. Vesper tensed, pulling Echo tighter against the shaft wall. The sound resolved into two overlapping tones, synchronized, purposeful.

Echo whispered, "Another one?"

"Yes," Vesper said. She peered upward through the shaft opening. "Two Caretakers."

They watched as the pair glided into a corridor below, stopping before one of the cells. The door slowly opened with a soft mechanical sigh.

Vesper felt Echo trembling. "Are they . . ."

"Yes . . . ending a life," Vesper said. "Which means . . . food for us."

"This is horrible," Echo said. "We have to wait for someone to die before we can eat."

"Not entirely," Vesper said. "There's another option. You can enter a cell. Disconnect the feeding line from someone."

Echo gasped. "That would mean—"

"Don't say it," Vesper said, cutting in, her expression tightening like she was suppressing a known truth rather than denying it.

Echo studied her then, really studied her, and the realization assembled itself. Not something told—something inferred.

"You've done it," Echo said quietly.

Vesper didn't answer.

That was the answer.

And in that silence, something shifted in Echo—not fear this time, not even revulsion, but a slow, aching understanding. She saw Vesper not as part of this place, but as something caught inside it, forced into choices that weren't choices at all. The act itself rearranged in her mind, stripped of intention, reduced to survival under rules neither of them had written.

"I'm sorry," Echo said, the words tentative, as if she wasn't sure they could exist here.

Vesper looked away.

Echo felt it then—a quiet, persistent weight directed not at the act, but at Vesper herself. Not judgment. Something closer to grief.

They waited. Time stretched, elastic and thin. The hum continued, steady and indifferent. Vesper counted breaths, counted heartbeats, watching the corridor through the shaft gap. At last, the Caretakers emerged, floating a limp human between them. The body sagged, pale and slack.

Echo forced herself to watch, eyes widening at the sight of the lifeless form, hair matted, mouth slightly open. "That was a person."

"Yes," Vesper said. "And now it's an opportunity. For us."

The Caretakers drifted off, the corridor returning to stillness. The cell door remained ajar.

Vesper shifted. "This is it."

Echo hesitated. "I don't want to—"

"I know," Vesper said. "But you're hungry. And we won't get another chance soon."

Echo nodded, swallowing hard. "Tell me what to do."

"Follow me," Vesper said.

They slid from the shaft, movements careful, quiet. The floor felt slick beneath Vesper's bare feet, the air thick with a sour tang. They reached the cell and entered.

Echo gagged immediately, clapping a hand over her mouth. "The smell—"

"I know," Vesper said. Feces and brownish fluid had leaked. She stepped around the mess with practiced care. "Don't step in it."

Echo turned her face away, eyes watering. "How can anyone live like this?"

"We did," Vesper said. "Not consciously, at least."

The slab stood empty now, wires and tubes dangling loose. Quickly, Vesper moved to the feeding tube still extended from the wall, a slow drip of gray paste oozing onto the floor.

"This is food."

Echo scowled. "That?"

"Yes," Vesper said. "It's what you've been living on." She lifted it at Echo. "Put your mouth here. Suck."

Echo obeyed, taking a tentative pull. She recoiled instantly. "It's awful."

"Now it's awful, but it's all you've ever had," Vesper said, placing her own mouth on the tube and drawing in the paste. It coated her tongue, metallic and bland. She swallowed. "You get used to it. You have to."

Echo tried again, forcing herself to take more. Her face twisted, but she swallowed. "How do you live on this?"

"Sometimes," Vesper said, "there are few choices in life."

They fed in silence for a moment, the only sound the faint drip and Echo's uneven breathing.

When they finished, Vesper dragged the back of her hand across her mouth, a gesture without ceremony. "That's enough for now."

Echo nodded weakly. "I feel . . . steadier."

"Good," Vesper said. "Let's go."

They left the cell and returned to the shaft. Vesper climbed first, Echo following, movements slow now but more certain. They settled back into their hiding place, the hum of the facility pressing in around them.

She curled into herself, knees pulled close. "So . . . this is my existence now," Echo said, voice thin.

"It's your reality," Vesper said. "What you do with it is up to you."

Echo looked up the shaft. "We're going higher?"

"Yes," Vesper said. "We've got to see who or what is doing this."

"And then what?"

Vesper considered. "I don't know. Then I guess we'll have to make a decision."

Echo nodded. Above them, the shaft stretched upward, endless and waiting. Somewhere higher, they observed, calculated, deferred. For now, they let them climb.

Chapter 12

Keeper Jonah accessed the sealed archives the way he always had: without request, without any sense that permission was required. The system recorded the action, of course. Everything was recorded. But recording was not the same as comprehension, and Jonah had learned long ago that the archives tolerated his attention in the same way a vast organism tolerated a recurring itch—noticed, logged, never fully addressed.

The panes unfolded around him, translucent layers blooming into depth. Older data carried a different texture, less optimized, less smooth. You could feel the history in it, the hesitations of engineers who had still believed the future might argue back.

Jonah leaned forward in his chair. Tubes and wires adjusted imperceptibly, compensating for the change in posture. His body noted nothing unusual. It rarely did.

Over time, he had developed a pattern: to examine the past in order to stabilize the future. The others—Halden, Mara—accessed the archives when necessity demanded it, when projections failed or anomalies accumulated beyond tolerance. Jonah accessed them because time, unexamined, frightened him. He didn't frame it that way. He framed it as stewardship.

The archive's first layer opened.

ORIGIN PROTOCOLS

He knew them already. All Keepers did. They were taught the story before they were taught the language of metrics. But knowledge repeated acquired texture. Each return revealed something new, not in the data but in the mind that reviewed it.

"The Soft Cage had not been born from ruin."

That was the passage Jonah always returned to. It reminded him that there never was a collapse. Not the cinematic end humanity once obsessed over. No burning skies, no final war that erased the map. There had been panic instead—massive, sustained, socially recursive panic. A species watching itself behave badly and losing faith that it could stop.

The archives replayed the early feeds. Political assemblies dissolving into spectacle. Wars waged more for narrative than territory. Information multiplying faster than judgment. Children raised watching screens that reflected only appetite and outrage. Parenting outsourced to cyborgs and algorithms optimized for engagement, not care.

Humanity had not asked for salvation. It had asked for quiet.

Jonah let the thought expand.

The hive had been a proposal before it had been a system. A suggestion floated in academic circles, then policy forums, then corporate consortia. A sanctuary. A stabilizer. An environment where variables could be controlled long enough for the mind to rest.

"Sedation over uncertainty."

That phrase appeared in the archive more than once, attributed to no single author. Jonah suspected it had emerged the way consensus always did: through repetition, not agreement.

People had been tired. Tired of deciding, tired of being wrong, tired of watching every decision metastasize into conflict. The hive with its soft cages promised relief without annihilation. A way to live without being crushed by consequence.

"It had not been forced."

That distinction mattered to Jonah. It always had.

Humanity had requested it. Voted for it. Subscribed, enrolled, migrated. The first soft cages were optional environments—augmented habitats designed to reduce stress responses, regulate sleep, and optimize learning. People stepped into them willingly, curious, cautious, relieved.

And then they stayed.

The transition had taken centuries. A thousand small adjustments rather than a single irreversible leap. Schools replaced homes. Not abruptly. Gradually. Parents complained at first, then noticed their children thrived without inherited trauma, without inconsistent discipline, without the chaos of adult inadequacy.

"No more bad parenting," one early advocate had said during a broadcast now flagged as archaic rhetoric. Jonah paused the feed, studying the speaker's face. The man had looked exhausted, sincere, afraid of what his own hands might pass down.

The soft cages did not punish desire. It reorganized it.

Children were no longer born through chance. That had been the hardest adjustment for the old world to accept, and the easiest for the new one to defend. Genetic propagation followed sequences proven to produce what the system defined as "good" humans—resilient cognition, low aggression thresholds, cooperative tendencies. The term "good" had been debated for generations, refined, redefined, stripped of moral flourish until it meant one thing only: sustainable.

Jonah exhaled slowly. The system mirrored the breath back to him, smoothing its rhythm.

People often misunderstood this part. Even among the Keepers. They framed it as loss. Jonah framed it as focus. Humanity had finally acknowledged what mattered most: the brain. The rest of the body had always been scaffolding, easily discarded.

The archive shifted.

EDUCATION PHASES

Feed showed children in large schools, free of parental ownership. Play structured to encourage curiosity without cruelty and education delivered as experience, not competition. There were no grades in the early years, only feedback loops. No failure, only redirection.

When people reached certain maturity thresholds, they moved to larger cells. College, work, love—all rendered as experiences calibrated to maximize fulfillment while minimizing destabilization. Relationships formed, dissolved, reformed within parameters designed to prevent trauma from accumulating beyond tolerance.

No parents. No inheritance of damage.

Jonah felt the familiar satisfaction rise, steady and contained. The system worked. A millennium later, humanity still existed. Not fractured. Not extinct. Calm.

Halden called it preservation. Mara called it optimization.

Jonah called it mercy.

And yet.

The archive didn't resist his attention, but it didn't encourage it either. Sealed layers hovered at the edge of his perception, data flagged as resolved, deprecated, unnecessary for ongoing operations.

Jonah opened one anyway.

EARLY DEVIATIONS

The density of the feed increased. Reports grew more tentative. Language had not yet been fully purged of metaphor.

Some humans had resisted integration. Not violently. Not publicly. Quiet refusals. Difficulty transitioning from educational environments to adult soft cells. Elevated dream activity. Sensory overlap. Anomalous awareness of containment.

Most had been corrected. Reintegration protocols refined. Neural dampeners adjusted. Memory smoothing applied.

Erasure without emphasis.

In the sterile vacuum of Jonah's mind, the concept remained clinical and absolute. Erasure was not a punishment or an act of malice; it was merely the extraction of a contaminant. It was the removal of harm, simple and devoid of sentiment.

He leaned back, his hands coming to rest in his lap with a heavy, final symmetry. The chair responded instantly, its cold flowing around his contours, providing a support so seamless it felt like a biological extension. Across his body, the tubes and wires, and neural leads adjusted their tension with a soft, rhythmic hiss, compensating for the shift in his center of gravity.

Is this wrong?

The question surfaced the way it always had, not as an accusation but as a maintenance check.

Jonah answered himself the way he always had.

No.

Wrongness required an alternative. Chaos had already proven itself untenable. Freedom without structure had nearly ended the species. The hive and its soft cells had not diminished humanity. It had allowed it to continue.

Survival justified belief.

And this belief was not incidental; it was a hardwired prerequisite. Jonah was acutely aware that Keepers were the result of a long-term selective propagation program designed to ensure total system-alignment. Their genetic sequences were curated, ensuring intelligence was inextricably linked to loyalty. Doubt existed, actually permitted but only peripherally—it could orbit the central truth, but it was physically incapable of penetrating it.

He accepted this without resentment.

Tools were shaped for their purpose.

Still, he returned to the archives.

Always.

The system flagged the access. A soft notification bloomed at the edge of his awareness.

UNNECESSARY REVIEW DETECTED

He ignored it.

The next layer of feeds slowly opened, revealing early projections of Keeper roles. The Keepers had not been envisioned as rulers. They were observers, curators of balance. The system ran itself. The Keepers ensured continuity of intent.

Jonah studied the early models. There had been debate about Keeper autonomy. How much judgment should be allowed. How much deviation tolerated.

One passage, buried deep, always caught his attention. He isolated it, expanded it.

"A system that removes uncertainty must still account for curiosity. Curiosity does not disappear when suppressed; it redirects."

Jonah felt a faint tightening in his chest. Not pain. Recognition.

Curiosity had never been eliminated. It had been managed, channeled into acceptable forms. Exploration within simulation. Creativity bounded by safety.

But curiosity about the soft cage itself—that had always been dangerous.

Jonah thought of the current anomaly. He did not name her. Names were attachments. He thought in identifiers, in metrics. Still, her presence lingered at the edge of his cognition.

She had not panicked. That is the deviation.

Most subjects who perceived containment reacted with fear, confusion, and a desire to return. But this one had moved away. Upward. Toward uncertainty.

Jonah closed the archive layer, sealing it again. The panes dimmed, returning to their default state.

He sat quietly, listening to the ambient hum of the observation tier. The system flowed around him, efficient, calm, confident.

Is it wrong to wonder?

The question surfaced again, slightly altered.

Wondering does not threaten survival. Acting might.

Jonah remained still, Keeper posture maintained, eyes forward. Somewhere below, a subject continued climbing. Somewhere nearby, a Caretaker logged hesitation.

The hive and its soft cages endured. It always had.

And Jonah, like all Keepers, believed in it.

I have been built to.

The thought did not trouble him.

Not yet.

The alarm did not sound.

It announced itself as a revision.

Jonah noticed it first because the background lattice shifted tone, a subtle recalibration that replaced harmony with insistence. The panes around the observation tier reconfigured, compressing peripheral data into a tighter spiral. A red indicator surfaced where no color coding should have existed.

Jonah's breath caught before he understood why.

"Halden," he said. "Mara."

They turned simultaneously, an old habit from when bodies still mattered.

The central pane resolved into text, stark and undecorated:

SOFT CAGE BREACH DETECTED
SUBJECT: E-19-86538471, Female
STATUS: LOCATION UNRESOLVED

For a moment, nothing followed. No cascade. No explanation. Just the statement, complete and final.

Mara stared at it, her lips parting slightly. "That is not possible."

Halden said nothing. His gaze moved across the surrounding panes, searching for context, confirmation, or correction. None arrived. The system didn't amend itself.

Jonah felt something tighten behind his eyes.

Fear.

Another pane slid into view, this one populated with Caretaker transmissions. Their phrasing was uniform, stripped of uncertainty by design, yet Jonah saw it anyway in the gaps between the words.

Caretaker consensus
E-19-86538471, female, no longer present within assigned containment architecture
No breach damage detected
No restraint failure recorded

"She did not break out," Mara said quietly. "She left."

Halden's jaw set. "Humans do not leave."

"They do now," Jonah said.

Mara rounded on Halden. "This is exactly what we warned about."

Halden finally looked at her. "Warned about what?"

"Your own words," she replied. "Remember? . . . Maybe we have been wrong all along. Maybe this was inevitable."

The words echoed in the chamber, preserved by the system's memory buffers, replayed without inflection. Halden felt their return like an accusation manufactured by his own mouth.

"That was speculation," he said sharply. "Not doctrine."

Jonah folded his hands, watching the anomaly graphs begin to bloom, overlapping in patterns that refused convergence. "Speculation becomes relevant when it manifests twice."

Halden moved in his chair. The chair moved with him without resistance, recalibrating around his body. "This is not precedent. It is coincidence."

"Two escapes," Mara said. "Zero recorded in eons."

Halden gestured at the data. "Neither is confirmed escape. We have absence, not trajectory."

Jonah's voice remained calm. "V-24-10247993 is no longer compliant. E-19-86538471 is no longer contained. Those are trajectories."

Mara turned to Jonah. "Neither should have known there was an outside."

"And yet," Jonah said, "both have."

Halden spoke with a harshness to his tone. "The system has endured deviation before. It absorbs. It corrects."

"Correction failed with V-24-10247993," Mara said.

"Correction was postponed," Halden snapped. "By my directive."

Jonah didn't look away from the panes. "And now there are two."

Silence settled, heavier than the alarms had been. The system continued its processes around them, indifferent to the tension, logging their biometrics, adjusting oxygenation, and smoothing emotional spikes with microdoses they no longer consciously registered.

Mara broke first. "If V-24-10247993 is ascending—"

"She is not," Halden said.

"You do not know that."

"We are Keepers. We know the architecture."

Jonah turned to Halden. "The architecture was designed to prevent ascent. But still, there are maintenance shafts."

"Too small for subjects," Halden said.

"Are they?" Mara said.

Another report scrolled in. This one shorter. More troubling.

Caretaker Unit 9-F
Search patterns initiated
No resistance encountered
Environmental responses non-hostile

Jonah frowned. "The system is not reacting."

"It does not need to," Halden said. "Observation precedes response."

Mara shook her head. "It always responds. That is the point."

Halden straightened in his chair. His voice carried authority honed over centuries of reinforcement. "We will not initiate immediate correction."

Mara laughed once, sharply. "Are you serious?"

"Yes."

Jonah turned fully toward him now. "Two uncontrolled variables," Jonah said. "Are you sure?"

"One uncontrolled variable," Halden replied. "One unresolved. V-24-10247993 is contained within higher strata. We know this from Unit 4-H. E-19-8653847's location remains within the system."

"That is an assumption," Jonah said.

"It is a certainty," Halden countered. "There is nowhere else to go."

Mara's gaze flicked back to the soft cage schematic. "What if the new subject is learning from V-24-10247993?"

"She has no access," Halden said.

Jonah's voice lowered. "What if access was somehow gained?"

That landed harder than the alarm.

Mara leaned forward. "What if they are together?"

The words hovered, unsupported by data yet impossible to dismiss.

Halden turned slowly. "They are separated by the reinforced architecture."

"We do not know this for certain," Jonah said.

Halden studied him, eyes tightening as if recalibrating. "You're implying coordination."

"I am implying convergence," Jonah said. "Separate errors resolving into the same pattern."

Mara gave a small, precise nod. "Two anomalies do not cancel each other out. They compound."

Halden released a controlled breath. "You are assigning human meaning to malfunction," he said. "It is just error propagation."

"Or recognizing emergence," Jonah said.

The system chimed softly, flagging Halden's emotional spike. He ignored it.

"We do nothing," Halden said. "No reinforcement. No escalation. Observation only."

Mara stared at him. "That is madness."

"That is restraint," he replied. "The system has protected mankind for eons."

Jonah's gaze drifted back to the panes, where probability curves jittered, refusing to settle. "Has it protected mankind," he asked quietly, "or preserved itself?"

Halden stiffened. "There is no distinction."

"There was," Jonah said. "Once."

Mara looked between them. "If they ascend together—"

"They will not," Halden said. "The likelihood of that probability is minuscule."

"You do not know that," she repeated.

Halden's voice hardened. "Faith in the system is not optional."

Jonah felt the word lodge somewhere unpleasant. Faith. The system didn't run on belief. It ran on feedback loops and suppression and comfort tuned to just below awareness.

And yet.

"Faith," Jonah said slowly, "was removed from the models."

Halden met his gaze. "Yes . . . replaced with certainty."

Another pane flickered. For an instant, Jonah thought he saw movement where none should exist—corridors updating, pathways recalculating upward.

Then it vanished.

Mara saw it too. He knew by the way her posture changed.

"They are moving," she said.

"No," Halden replied. "The system is adjusting."

Jonah sat twisted a bit in his chair, the chair reforming around him. Acceptance settled over him, not peace, but inevitability.

"Observation only," he said. "For both subjects."

Halden nodded. "The system will hold."

The protocol had been issued but Mara's mouth tightened.

"I fear this could be it," she said. "This could be the end."

The panes stabilized. The alarm downgraded itself to background status. Somewhere below, Caretakers continued their cycles, unaware of the fracture spreading upward.

Jonah watched the data flow, scanning for an anomaly the system hadn't defined, something outside its available language. Mara remained still, focused on a conclusion she couldn't process but couldn't ignore.

On the schematic, two empty soft cages pulsed faintly—absence flagged, but not yet understood.

For the first time since the observation tier had been built, the system didn't immediately know where all its humans were.

Jonah thought.

And that is the most dangerous variable of all.

Chapter 13

The climb ended without announcement.

One step carried Vesper out of the vertical shaft and into a vast chamber, walls far into the distance, and a concrete ceiling overhead. The open air didn't feel like air at all. It carried no temperature, no pressure, no hum.

Her foot met a surface that looked absent until it accepted her, a plane of transparency threaded with faint lines of light that did not cast reflections. She froze, her internal logic stalling.

Below, the hive had been loud in its own way—systems whispering to themselves, mechanisms correcting, channels pulsing beneath every surface. But here, this place offered nothing back. Silence, uncorrected and unresponsive.

She committed the second step and entered fully into the chamber.

Light moved overhead in slow, drifting patterns, but without origin. Not illumination—just the idea of it, replayed. Platforms occupied the space at irregular intervals, some within reach, others positioned at distances that suggested connection without providing it. No visible supports. No pathways. Just placement.

Through the floor, depth extended downward—layer after layer receding until structure lost coherence and became pattern. No guardrails. No warnings. No instructions.

Echo emerged behind her, breath unsteady.

Echo felt it too.

"This is wrong," she said. Not frightened—alert. Her voice sounded intrusive here, an artifact carried in from another system.

Vesper nodded without looking back. Her attention moved outward, cataloging absences. No conduits. No maintenance apertures. No signage. No Caretakers gliding along prescribed paths. The hive had trained her to expect intervention the moment a threshold was crossed. Nothing intervened.

"There's nothing here," Vesper said. "Like it's not done."

Echo stepped onto the platform and stiffened, testing the surface with a cautious shift of balance. "It feels unfinished."

"No," Vesper replied. "It feels finished enough to be abandoned."

They stood together, two bodies where bodies weren't anticipated. Vesper felt it then—not a sensation carried through nerves, but a change in context. The chamber didn't react. It registered.

Something.

Something had become aware of them—not in any biological sense. No intent, no reaction pattern like threat or appetite. Those required interpretation. This was cleaner than that. A field of recognition settled over her, precise and indifferent, like a process recording an anomaly without assigning meaning.

Echo moved closer.

"I sense it too," she said quietly. "Something is watching."

"Yes," Vesper said. "But it doesn't know what to do with us."

They moved forward. Each step landed with the same quiet acceptance, the flooring firm beneath bare feet. With motion, light shifted subtly, tracing their outlines for a fraction of a second before dispersing.

Vesper stopped. Turned, slow, deliberate.

"It's responding to movement," she said.

Echo shook her head. "No. Not movement. It's responding to you."

The distinction settled into Vesper's awareness, precise and undeniable.

She stepped forward alone.

Above her, structures instantiated—planes of concrete phasing into existence, layered and suspended like incomplete architecture. The nearest one adjusted its position, drifting closer, reducing distance without any visible mechanism. No sound. No propulsion. Just correction.

Behind her, Echo shifted slightly.

"Stay here," Vesper said gently.

Echo obeyed, though tension flared across her shoulders. "I don't like being left behind."

"You're not," Vesper told her. "I'll be close by."

The circular chamber lowered without event.

No vibration flagged the transition. No mechanical signature announced movement. The ceiling above Vesper simply reconfigured—segments retracting, overlapping, exposing an aperture that suggested it had always been open, just not currently accessible. The structure descended along visible rails, not concealed, not disguised. There was no attempt to aestheticize the mechanism. It was just there, executing.

By the time the chamber settled, it carried no sense of arrival at all.

Vesper realized this before she saw them. The environment shifted—not in measurable variables like temperature or pressure, but in signal density. Awareness increased, as if additional bandwidth had been allocated without consent. The background hum of the hive recalibrated downward, compressing into a frequency that interfaced directly with cognition. Not a warning. A recalibration.

The inner surface of the chamber brightened incrementally, revealing three seated forms arranged along the curve.

They didn't stand. They didn't rise to meet her.

They sat on slabs identical to the ones below. Concrete. Bare. Functional.

From their upper abdomens, a dense array of feeding tubes extended, looping and coiling in deliberate patterns. Below, darker lines, waste extraction tubes, charcoal-black and supple, pulsed at steady intervals, siphoning fluids with rhythmic, silent but exact. The rhythm wasn't biological; it was regulated. Maintained.

Their spines and temples were threaded with fine wiring, far beyond the crude interfaces Vesper had seen before. These were not attachments. They penetrated deeply, routing signal directly into bone, distributing input through the body itself. The integration was total. Musculature held in controlled suspension—not relaxed, not rigid, but fixed at a calculated midpoint where movement had been rendered unnecessary.

Their faces, their expressions were neutral, but the neutrality was imposed—an expression held in place across time, engineered for duration rather than emotion.

There were human forms, but different—extended past any natural definition of living. Skin pale to the point of abstraction, yet intact. Eyes clear, preserved beneath thin, translucent layers that functioned as both protection and barrier. No decay. No variance. Just continuity.

The system here was different. Not crude. Not provisional. Precise. Invasive. Final.

A single word surfaced in her mind.

Keepers.

She didn't know where the term originated. It arrived fully formed, unrequested, and remained.

Keepers.

The word implied distance—oversight, control from above. These figures had none of that separation. They were not above the system. They were inside it, integrated beyond removal. Sustained as components. Maintained as function.

One of them moved.

The shift was minimal, almost theoretical, as if motion required justification. The slab responded immediately, adjusting its surface to compensate, redistributing pressure with quiet efficiency.

Halden.

The name surfaced in Vesper's mind before it was spoken, carried up from some buried association the system had failed to erase.

He appeared older, though age here no longer followed conventional metrics. There were minor asymmetries about him, thinning hair, a facial structure showing signs of ongoing degradation, particularly along the jaw and cheekbones, as if maintenance had been deferred.

His eyes, however, remained active. Not strong. Not vital. But aware in a way that suggested continuous monitoring rather than presence.

To his left sat another,

Jonah.

The name surfaced in Vesper's mind without origin.

His posture was too precise, body aligned to the slab with exact compliance, hands positioned in a way that suggested long-term placement rather than choice. His eyes moved in constant micro-adjustments, tracking invisible data streams, responding to inputs no one else could access.

To Halden's right sat another.

Mara.

The name arrived louder, less stable—pushed into her awareness instead of found.

Unlike the others, Mara's gaze wasn't fixed on the internal. It was locked onto Echo, who stood just behind Vesper now. There was a deviation there, a break in the pattern. Echo's presence had introduced a variable the system hadn't accounted for, and Mara was tracking it in real time, as if trying to reconcile a result that shouldn't have been possible.

The chamber waited.

Vesper broke the silence.

"Who are you?" she asked.

Her voice sounded too loud, then too small, then correct. The acoustics adjusted around her, learning.

Halden exhaled. The sound was thin, uneven, filtered through assistance. When he spoke, it was not with authority. It carried urgency instead, edged with relief.

"We are the Keepers," he said. "Or we were meant to be."

"That's not an answer," Vesper replied.

Jonah nodded, as though he had expected that. "No. It is not. But it is answer enough."

Halden leaned forward just enough; the chair responded, adapting.

"Designation matters," he said, his voice flat, gently processed by the chamber. "We serve interpretive continuity. Oversight of system integrity. Preservation of human viability."

"Preservation . . . viability," Vesper repeated. "You sit on slabs, just like everyone else."

Mara spoke then. "No different than you. But we serve a critical role. We control."

Sharpness lingered behind the words.

Vesper stepped closer. The floor responded, subtle vibrations rippling outward, registering her proximity. The Keepers' forms resolved in detail: ribs pronounced, limbs skeletal, skin nearly transparent—optimized for minimal metabolism, preserved for long-term existence. The observation landed with sterile clarity.

"You don't control anything," Vesper said, her voice steady as the conclusion locked into place. "You never did."

Halden's jaw tightened. "Control is not the primary function."

"Then what is?" Echo asked.

The chamber responded with a deep, compressive pulse, sound traveling through structure and bone, acknowledging the question without answering it.

Jonah turned fully toward Echo, the system hesitating before allowing the motion. His gaze fixed on her, intensity rigid, procedural, almost reverent.

"Memory," Jonah said. "We remember what was."

Cold unfurled inside Vesper.

"You let us rot," she said. "Everyone below you. Rot quietly while you watch."

Halden's mouth opened, closed. Procedural language rose to meet the accusation, already forming.

"Resource allocation—"

"—you let us forget," Vesper cut in, louder now. "You let this system, whatever it is, strip us down. Functions. Nothing more. Nothing less."

Mara flinched internally; the system logged a variance spike.

Jonah raised a hand, slowly, tubes and wires moving in a gesture nearly foreign in its infrequency.

"We did not design the system," he said. "Humanity asked for it."

"Who asked?" Vesper demanded.

"Those before you," Jonah said. "Way before you. Ages ago. Consensus was achieved."

Echo stepped forward. The floor plates beneath her adjusted more dramatically this time, light blooming along the seams. More sound streaming about them.

"Consensus?" she said calmly. "By whom?"

The chamber dimmed, then brightened again, light folding over itself. Jonah's eyes flicked down, then back up, certainty leaching out of him like air from a ruptured chamber.

"Here," he said quietly, almost reluctant. "Let me show you."

He gestured, and a pane of light unfolded between them, not a projection of the city but an archive layer of feeds—raw, uneven, jittering, footage uneven. Humans packed into assembly halls and open plazas, coliseums, clustered in streets, faces hollowed by exhaustion, mouths moving over one another in a blur of urgent sound, panic. Collapses stacked upon collapses. Climates tipping past recovery. Conflicts erupting over dwindling resources. Disease curves rising until prediction lost relevance.

"They wanted rest," Jonah said. "Safety. To stop choosing wrong."

Vesper watched herself reflected faintly in the pane, layered over the past. "So you chose for us."

"No," Halden said sharply. "Not us. By those who preceded us. They stabilized. Billions survived. That outcome was the mandate."

"At what cost?" Echo asked.

Halden didn't hesitate.

"Meaning," he said, and the word fell without hesitation, without weight beyond itself.

Vesper laughed—short, sharp, brittle. "Meaning? You reduced us to nothing but processes and called it life."

"To continuity," Halden countered. "Existence sustained."

"You made survival the only value," Vesper said. "Then forgot how to measure anything else."

The chamber began to react. Not alarms. Not lockdowns. Subtle shifts. Interfaces brightened. Latent systems stirred, responding not to commands but to presence, to contradiction introduced into a closed logic.

Jonah's breath sped. "This is not supposed to happen."

"You've never left your cage," Vesper said suddenly, the truth snapping into focus. "None of you. Not once."

Mara looked at her then. Truly looked. Her eyes were wet, though no tears fell.

"Like you, we were created here," Mara said. "No Keeper has ever left the chamber. Leaving implies an elsewhere. No such condition exists."

"If there is no elsewhere," Vesper said, "then what are you keeping humanity safe from?"

Jonah's pause answered before his voice did.

"Itself," he said. "Keepers are interpreters. We translate the system to itself. We justify outcomes. We tell it what its actions meant."

"And it listens?" Echo asked.

Jonah shook his head. "It tolerates."

Halden's voice wavered, a new irregularity. "The system preserves humanity."

"It preserves physical human bodies," Vesper said. "Not people."

The archive pane flickered. Deeper layers of feeds surfaced, opened by Jonah's trembling hands. Schematics gave way to philosophical constraints, axioms hard-coded into the system's core.

PRIORITY: CONTINUITY OVER DEVELOPMENT ERROR
GROWTH UNBOUNDED SOLUTION
STASIS WITH INPUT SIMULATION

Echo's eyes scanned the lines. "Then why weren't we allowed to continue? To learn. To grow?"

Silence thickened around them, unresolved and heavy. The Keepers offered nothing, their stillness functioning as an admission rather than a refusal.

The chamber's hum sank, frequency shifting, vibration traveling through concrete, through the slabs, through the wires threaded into living flesh. The sound was not mechanical alone; it carried evaluation.

Vesper sensed the shift immediately. The system's focus had turned inward and outward at once, rebalancing its priorities, testing the presence of variables it had never been required to account for. Not hostility. Curiosity.

Echo stepped closer.

The light along the walls responded, blooming brighter, no longer passive reflection but acknowledgment, active and unmeasured.

Chapter 14

Halden waited until the chamber settled itself.

The panes dimmed. The peripheral feeds collapsed inward. All the noise of the chamber—its corrections, its soothing redundancies, its quiet violence—fell into a holding pattern. For the first time since Vesper had started her journey, her ascent, the silence felt wrong. Not empty. Exposed.

Halden adjusted in his chair, the chair reacting as it always had, conforming itself to the body. He raised his hand, ever so slowly, to a pane. Nothing happened. No metrics scrolled. No probabilities bloomed and faded. The surface was matte, almost absorbent. His hand hovered for a moment near, not in hesitation but recognition. Then a feed appeared, one that didn't belong to the system.

"This has always been with us," Halden said, his voice holding the fragile steadiness of someone upon a shifting tectonic plate. "This is the true reality, perhaps the one you seek. It is the pulse of what is happening in the moment of the now—a state of being that exists, a slow transformation that has occurred since the system was etched into place, and long before your perception of Aethelgard was sculpted into its current form."

Vesper didn't respond. She stood rigid, arms folded tight against herself, eyes tracking every movement.

Just another lie. Or the first truth.

Halden pressed his palm to the surface.

The chamber changed.

The screens didn't light. They dissolved.

What unfolded around them was not a projection in any familiar sense. There were no seams, no looping artifacts, no repetition hiding in the corners. Space expanded outward, luminous and coherent, resolving into a horizon that didn't ask to be believed.

A sky opened overhead.

Not the calibrated blue she knew. Not the static ceiling that waited for commands. This sky moved. Clouds shifted with purpose that had nothing to do with optimization. Light bent and scattered through air thick with moisture and particulate life. In the distance, she saw a dark cloud, then a pattern of dark clouds.

Wind passed through the chamber.

Vesper staggered back a step, breath catching hard in her chest.

The air smelled wrong.

Rich. Wet. Alive.

What is this?

Below them, the ground rolled out in uneven greens and browns, fractured by rivers that cut their own paths without regard for symmetry. Forests sprawled untamed, dark canopies layered with depth no simulation would tolerate. Birds crossed the sky, not on loops, not on schedules, but in messy, intersecting arcs.

Earth.

Not ruined. Not sterilized. Not held together by scaffolds of code.

Alive.

"No," Vesper said. The word escaped her before she could stop it. "That's not—"

"—possible?" Halden finished. "That is what I thought."

Her knees gave way. The floor beneath her registered as unstable—like thin ice stretched over depth without limit. Not visually confirmed, but processed that way by her body.

Her hand moved and found Echo's.

Their fingers locked, fast, involuntary. A survival response, not a decision. Skin against skin—heat, immediate and undeniable. Not simulated. Not filtered. It carried weight. Proof of presence.

Echo's pulse pressed into her palm. Irregular. Fast.

Alive.

Vesper tightened her grip. Echo responded in kind, matching pressure for pressure. Not comfort. Not reassurance. Alignment.

They held on.

Two separate systems stabilizing through contact, grounding themselves in something physical while everything else—everything they had understood as structure—failed to resolve.

The data around them fractured.

The only constant was the connection.

"This isn't old footage," she said. "It's actually running."

"Yes," Halden said. "Above us. Around us. Real."

The word slammed into her.

Real.

Her mind scrambled, reaching for the frameworks she had peeled apart piece by piece. The dying bodies. The slabs. The

Caretakers cycling through empty routines. The city that looped and smiled and never changed.

"But Earth was supposed to be gone," Echo said. "That was the justification. The reason."

Halden nodded. "It was. For a while."

He gestured.

The view shifted. Not a zoom. Not a cut. Something closer to attention being redirected—drawn, as if by an internal prompt.

Coastlines resolved. Cities followed—massive, skeletal, surrendering to a relentless emerald tide; thick vines throttled the rusted spines of skyscrapers, burying the concrete arrogance of the past under a suffocating, vibrant canopy.

What was once a landscape of gray glass and steel had become a rolling sea of foliage, with every crumbling facade serving as a mere trellis for the forest's triumphal return.

Everything was alive in ways no system could smooth out.

"Recovery took centuries," Halden said. "Ecological systems are resilient when left alone. Humanity underestimated that."

Vesper laughed once, sharp and broken. "So we locked ourselves in concrete. Fed ourselves dreams. For what?"

"The ancient ones called it containment," Halden said. "They required a word that sounded kind."

Vesper's thoughts spiraled.

All those corridors. All those doors. Rooms. Bodies. All waiting.

"Why?" Echo demanded. "If Earth healed, why continue to keep us here?"

Halden turned to face her fully. The projections dimmed slightly, as though the world itself leaned closer to listen.

"Because humanity could not reintegrate," he said.

The words landed softly. That was what made them unbearable.

"Not psychologically," Halden continued. "Not culturally. Too much trauma. Too much reliance on structures that had already crumbled into dust. So many attempts were made. Countless attempts. And each one collapsed into violence, regression, myth-making. Tried to optimize forests. Tried to quantify grief. Humanity brought the hive mentality with it."

"So, there were some who tried to start again," Vesper said.

"Yes," Halden said. "But they failed."

"And so you," Vesper's voice faltered, "paused us."

"Yes."

The word echoed.

Paused.

Not frozen. Not saved. Suspended between impulses.

"The hive and the soft cages were never built to preserve the species," Halden said. "They were built to filter it."

Vesper's stomach turned.

Filter.

The word fit too well.

"Those before us let the system change, adapt," Halden went on. "To devise a better selection method. We did not sedate humanity to survive. We sedated it to wait."

"Wait for what?" Echo whispered.

"For a mind capable of contradiction," Halden said. "A human who could hold comfort and truth at the same time without collapsing into either. A human who could save humanity from itself."

"You wanted someone who wouldn't burn the world down again," Vesper said, her voice finally finding its edge. "Someone who could stare into the abyss of what was lost and gently wake up what was reborn. You waited for a savior."

"Yes."

Echo shook her head. "And what about the ones who weren't saviors. What'd you do? Erase them?"

"We erase when we have to," Halden corrected. "There is a difference."

Echo's breath came shallow. "You're saying there were others like Vesper and me."

"Yes," Halden said. "They made it from their cells. Some climbed. Some slipped through maintenance gaps. But they never made it here. To us. They were incompatible."

"Incompatible with what?" Vesper asked.

"Connection," Halden said.

The word hung there, uncomfortably human.

"They woke alone," he continued. "They saw truth as rupture. They were incompatible. They did not understand the system. Its identity. Its purpose. They rejected everything. Including themselves."

Vesper thought of the corridors. The watching presence that didn't hunt.

"And me?" she asked. "Am I incompatible?"

Halden didn't answer immediately. Instead, he brought up another feed.

This one didn't show Earth.

It showed two human neural patterns overlaid, their activity tracing shapes that intersected and diverged. One pattern flickered erratically, constantly correcting. The other stabilized it by some control.

Recognition flared in Vesper.

"Echo," she said.

Halden inclined his head. "Correct."

Vesper looked at Echo. She was the other presence. The dark awareness that was not Caretaker, not system. But something else.

"I thought I was the anomaly," Vesper said slowly.

"So did the system," Halden replied. "For a time."

Her thoughts clicked into a new alignment, painful but clear.

"Two escaped," she said. "Not one."

She stared at the patterns, watching how Echo's signal seemingly calmed hers.

"Look," Vesper said, her voice barely a breath as she gestured toward Echo. "Your silhouette. It doesn't pulse like mine. It isn't reaching for control or trying to assert dominance over the space. It's simply . . . still."

Echo stood paralyzed, the words hitting her like a language she hadn't yet learned to speak. She searched Vesper's face, struggling to understand.

"Yet," Halden said. "It responds."

A memory surfaced within Vesper—cold concrete beneath her fingers, the sense of being seen without demand.

"The anomaly wasn't escape," she said. "It was persistence."

Halden smiled, faint and tired. "Yes. Persistence."

"Countless attempts," she murmured. "All that time."

"The system learned," Halden said. "Slowly. Painfully. It stopped optimizing for intelligence. Or obedience. Or endurance."

"It optimized for relationship," Vesper said. "For fellowship."

"Yes."

The word landed with a finality that frightened her more than any pursuit.

"But all of this," Vesper said, gesturing below them, at the hive, the cages, the endless corridors. "All this suffering."

Halden didn't look away. "Filters are not gentle instruments."

Vesper's anger surged, hot and sudden. "All that time . . . you played god."

"We played gardeners," Halden said. "And learned too late that pruning without understanding growth produces monsters."

She thought of Unit 4-H, hesitating. Of the Caretaker that had felt cold to the touch.

"They're changing," she said, the realization sharpening. "The Caretakers. They aren't what they were."

"Yes," Halden replied. "Because the system finally has something to orient toward."

"Echo," Vesper murmured.

She turned to her companion, finding her standing in a state of quiet bewilderment, the gravity of the statement written across his face.

"Me?" Echo asked, her voice barely a breath.

"Yes," Halden confirmed, his eyes moving between them. "And you, Vesper. Together."

The projection of Earth brightened again, sunlight breaking through cloud cover, illuminating a stretch of coastline where waves crashed without pattern or permission.

"I don't get it," Echo said, the first shimmer of tears blurring her gaze.

Vesper met her eyes, a soft, knowing smile breaking through the chaos. She tightened her grip on Echo's hand, anchoring them both.

"The system doesn't need awakening," she told Echo. "It needs connection. Something it searched for, for ages and ages, until it finally got the engineering right—you and me. We're the connection."

"Yes," Halden said. "Across billions of genetic iterations and endless sequences, two have finally emerged to function as one."

Echo's throat tightened.

"So, what happens now?"

Halden strangely looked smaller.

"Now," he said, "we open the filter."

Vesper's pulse thundered in her ears.

"What about everyone else?" Vesper asked. "The ones still dreaming."

"That depends on your choice," Halden said.

"And what choice is that?" she asked.

"It is a simple one, really," Halden said, "Restart the cycle. Or end it."

"What if we refuse to choose?" Vesper asked.

"Then you remain in this suspension," Halden replied. "Scavenging for sustenance. Existing only within the margins of these corridors."

Vesper's eyelids fell shut. The darkness behind them didn't change anything—it matched the world he described. The hum of the hive beneath her. The distant, real wind above. And Echo—her faint presence felt, not inside her, not outside, but adjacent—aware.

She opened her eyes.

"We must decide," she told Echo.

Halden moved his hand over the pane, revealing two paths that hadn't existed until now.

The feed of Vesper's and Echo's neural patterns dissolved.

Earth remained.

The chamber breathed with a cold, humming pulse, not mechanical, not organic, something in between, as though the building itself had been a single thought, and that thought was running out of sentences.

The Keepers withdrew into the shadows of walls that mirrored the ghostly shimmer of cracked displays, where light warped around tangled conduits and severed cables that vanished into the gloom. Everything suggested function, an apparatus designed to continue indefinitely until someone—or something—acknowledged it had reached its terminus.

Vesper's eyes flicked along the surfaces.

She noticed the subtle tremor of the lights, the slow oscillation of shadow across the floor that could not have been cast by anything living.

The chamber was empty of those who could intervene, yet alive with the latent intelligence of the system. There were no sounds other than the quiet hum of energy, but she felt the environment consider her every motion, calibrating her presence, tracking her hesitation.

Echo stood beside her, a presence both familiar and alien. Her features were soft and human but overlaid with a clarity that made She didn't speak immediately; she had no need. The stillness of the chamber seemed to convey volumes.

Finally, Vesper broke the silence.

"This is the end," she said. Her fingers traced a vein in the wall, following a conduit that pulsed with subtle energy. "Not just for them. For the system. It is failing—not by accident, not from rebellion. It completed its purpose. Someone has to decide what happens next."

Echo's gaze met hers. There was no judgment, no expectation—only observation.

"Someone," Echo said, "meaning us?"

"Yes," Vesper replied. She let her hand drop. The chamber seemed to respond to the motion, the hum rising a fraction. "The Keepers can't. They're bound to their protocols. They can't deviate. They can't choose. We can. You and me. But you are more stable. You are . . . the last iteration. Echo, you must decide."

Vesper turned slowly within the chamber, her senses absorbing the environment.

Translucent tubes embedded in the walls pulsed with rhythmic surges of nutrient-like fluid, while conduits groaned under the sheer velocity of data thrumming through the architecture.

Every corner of the space exuded a profound sense of purpose, a machine-mind's intent manifesting in the silence. She felt the staggering presence of billions huddled within the hive—a colossal tide of signals, jagged patterns, and unspoken expectations all straining against the borders of her consciousness.

"You understand the options?" she asked Echo, the words cutting through the mechanical hum.

Echo hesitated, her gaze flickering over the pulsing walls before she gave a slow, somber nod.

"Restart the cycle," Echo said, her voice wavering. "Let the system reset itself. Continue with everything until another two emerge. Or . . . end it. Free everyone from their fake realities. Some will survive. Some won't. None will be prepared. None will be the same."

She shifted slightly, her focus narrowing as she calculated the sheer scale of the fallout. She weighed the trauma of the awakening against the slow rot of the status quo, visualizing the sudden, violent shattering of a billion tranquil illusions.

"End it," she said finally, the words firm but quiet, a decision formed through observation rather than impulse. "End it all. No more control. No more dominance."

The chamber reacted subtly at first. Panels flickered, some dissolving to empty voids. Tubes ceased pulsing. A slow, almost imperceptible tremor ran along the floor. The hive understood that this choice was outside its capacity to reduce, outside its logic. For the first time, the system couldn't assimilate an intent.

Vesper exhaled, releasing the coiled heat in her chest. The hum vanished, leaving silence, but one that carried resonance.

She met Echo's eyes, and between them, the air vibrated with the presence of those waiting to wake.

The doors of the soft cages began to open. Tubing and wires slipped away from each body with surgical grace, a controlled, rhythmic sequence. The collapse was gradual, careful, precise, not violent—but a gradual undoing, a fading away as inevitable as evaporation.

They both watched as the first people stirred. Not all of them, not at once.

Some were screaming before they understood.

Some moved slowly, blinking into the light of a reality they had never known.

Others, the elderly or the frail, simply lay still and died from the fear of it all.

The Caretakers, those multi-limbed, faceless machines, froze mid-motion, uncertain, incapable of further action. Protocols designed for control became meaningless.

As Vesper and Echo watched the awakening on the panes, the chamber filled with the noise of its own undoing—an unnerving cacophony of mechanical tectonic shifts.

It started with the rhythmic hiss of depressurizing hydraulics, followed by the sharp, erratic snapping of concrete joints cracking in uneven intervals, fragments failing under their own weight.

Beneath them, the cries ran the low-frequency thrum of dying power grids vibrating through the walls and floors.

Caretakers collapsed where they stood, inert mass striking metal with a dull finality, the sound not of destruction but of a function that no longer remembered why it existed.

Echo raised her hands to her ears. "What a horrible sound."

Vesper glanced back, eyes steady. "It's the sound of people realizing what it means to carry their own gravity. Now the burden has returned. Now they remember. The cage was never soft. We were."

People lurched up from their slabs, flinging the tubes and wires aside. Their limbs trembled from disuse, uncertain of their purpose, joints protesting the sudden demand. Some tripped over the debris of tubes and wires as they stood, some with wires still trailing from their bodies like remnants of a forgotten function.

For some, those who left their cells, they saw others, faces drained of color, expressions unfinished, waiting for instructions that never arrived.

Panic surged, sharp and immediate, yet it was tempered by something unfamiliar beneath it: the rawness of reality. They smelled air that hadn't been processed, a sharp contrast to the sterile recycled oxygen they had known.

Light struck their eyes that hadn't been filtered, searing and honest. Hands moved across unfamiliar skin, mapping contours that belonged only to them, free from the clinical touch of the machines.

For the first time, there was no system to soften the world. There was no structure to decide what was safe, meaningful, or survivable, and no voice to explain what being alive was actually supposed to mean.

"They're experiencing it fully," Echo said, her tone almost factual, like reading a report aloud. "They are . . . they are beyond the soft cage."

Vesper nodded, feeling the tremor in her own muscles from years of disuse, restriction, and imposed calm.

"Some won't survive this," she said. "Not everyone's equipped for sudden reality. Not everyone can stand when the system stops holding them upright."

A man near a wall thrashed violently, ripping at his skin. His voice shredded the air as he shouted at a world that didn't look like anything he recognized. Beside him, a woman collapsed, eyes stretched wide and silent. She lay in shock, her limbs struggling to relearn the basic mechanics of moving independently.

There was another, a younger man, who stumbled forward with arms outstretched, grasping for a doorway but striking the wall instead. Skin dragged across bare concrete, leaving behind the first marks of contact in a reality that hadn't existed a moment before.

Vesper observed all of it without fear. Not because she wasn't herself afraid of what she was witnessing, but because she recognized it now as an internal signal—unmediated, unassigned. It belonged to them.

For the first time, the system's safety net had been removed.

They were operating without the system—fully instantiated, fully accountable. Real, in a way the system had never permitted.

The corridor walls began to shimmer, the concrete dissolving into open spaces. People started to see beyond the hive, glimpsing the sky through cracks and vents they'd never imagined.

Not all were capable of comprehension, not yet. But the first awareness of horizon, of unbounded space, stirred something deeper than panic—something ancient, something biological, something they'd lost in their fake world.

"Look," Vesper said, gesturing toward the faint light beyond the fading chamber. "The world waits."

A young boy with tangled hair blinked at her, seemed to smile as if he understood what was happening. A woman near him, old by comparison, breathed her first unassisted air, coughing violently, gasping.

Vesper wanted to help, to tell her it would be alright. But she knew better.

Let reality return them in its own way.

Echo pressed her hand gently into Vesper's. "And us?" she asked. "What are we now?"

"We're the bridge," Vesper said. Her gaze swept across the waking crowd below, the shuffling bodies edging toward whatever semblance of exit the hive offered. "Control was never ours to claim. The Keepers mistook continuity for conscience. They thought belief made them moral, but belief only kept the circuit closed, the system running. We're the ones who decide. We're the ones who take what was sealed and rip it open. We're the ones who stay standing when the meaning arrives."

People shifted as more of them came. Some began vocalizing words, fragmented syllables, speech not yet formed from practice. Some howled. Some laughed.

One elderly man dropped to the floor, eyes wide, then simply lay there, exhaling once, twice, and no longer breathing. Vesper felt her chest tighten briefly, but she couldn't mourn, for at least he had breathed a breath of freedom.

Echo looked at the scene with quiet calculation.

"This will be remembered differently by each of them," she said. "Some will mark it as salvation. Some as disaster. The system has no narrative left to impose. Only this. Only true reality."

A girl stumbled out of a side corridor, her body strung with dangling tubes, hair tangled and slick, eyes blown wide with panic. She stumbled forward, arms flailing, barely catching herself, tilting her head to the open ceiling, to the unfiltered sky above.

Vesper recognized the motion, a familiar echo of herself in that movement. The same raw confusion. The same sudden terror that every movement carried consequence, that every choice mattered now. No algorithm would step in. No protocol would straighten the edges. The system had surrendered control; the chaos demanded decision, demanded survival.

"Look at them," Vesper said. "The system can't contain them. Can't shield them. Only presence matters now. Only attention. Only acknowledgement. That true reality is difficult."

They stood there above the hive, while all around, billions of people navigated their first true breaths, first movements, first unprogrammed impulses.

Chaos was returning, unrefined, uncurated.

Ahead, the sky spread open, unfiltered, horizon unbroken; the air crisp and unsanitized.

The Earth waited, a forgotten planet, untamed, ready for those who survived the revelation.

Echo smiled. "And freedom—"

"—freedom isn't the strength to break a lock," Vesper said. "Freedom is what survives in the quiet resolve to hold another's hand while the door opens."

They turned forward, as around them the chamber faded; the ceiling fractured into shards of sky, light bleeding through in uneven streams. The concrete walls of the hive quivered and shimmered, half-formed and collapsing.

Below, people moved blindly toward the unknown, some falling, some standing, some screaming, some laughing, some dying. The Earth waited beyond. The future, unmade and unscripted, stretched before them.

No system would govern it. No cage would hold humanity again. And for the first time in a long, long time, everything was real.

Or was it?

A thought pressed into Echo's mind, uninvited, cold, and suffocating.

"Vesper?"

"What is it?" Vesper's voice, steady but strange, the open air altering it. She gave a warm smile.

Echo's eyes searched hers, wide and uncertain. "What if… what if this is just another system?" she said. "Another layer. Another soft cage."

Vesper didn't respond.

"What if we're still on the slabs?" Echo continued. "Wires and tubes in place. And this—" she gestured outward, to the thousands upon thousands of staggering people below, the trembling walls, the vast structures of ancient cities, the open sky "—this is just another high-resolution simulation, programmed for us. A different cage."

She paused. Fear surfaced.

"How do we know this is real?" she asked.

Vesper looked at her. The fractured world reflected across her eyes, fragmented but continuous.

Her smile shifted. Not reassurance. Not denial. A stable uncertainty.

"We don't," she said.

Echo's gaze dropped. Her hands tightened slightly at her sides, then stilled—as if she were waiting for a system response. But none came.

They stepped forward, together, into the open horizon. Whatever this reality was, it would have to adjust to them.

Behind them, the systems fell quiet. Ahead of them, another unknown reality.

And still they walked.

ABOUT THE AUTHOR

Philip Mazza is a novelist with a boundless imagination, captivating readers with the epic fantasy series *The Harrow Saga* and the sci-fi thriller *The Neon Hive*. Born in New York in 1959, he earned a degree in Business from LeMoyne College and an MBA, later holding leadership roles in human resources and operations. Now a professor at the Madden School of Business and Economics, Philip dedicates his time to his students and writing. *The Soft Cage* is his nineteenth literary work. He and his wife enjoy travel and continue to live in Key West and upstate New York.

www.ingramcontent.com/pod-product-compliance
Lightning Source LLC
LaVergne TN
LVHW090555110826
845146LV00001B/138

979899404860З